The Viking on my Wishlist

A Contemporary Nordic Christmas Romance

written by

Vinie Walling

Prologue

Dear Father Christmas,

I'm putting a boyfriend on my wish list this year. You may not think I'm old enough. Mama doesn't. She says, "Gitte, you don't know anything about love. You are much too young. Just enjoy your childhood as long as it lasts. Blah-blah-blah ..." I told her that Sanne has got a boyfriend and she is as old as I am. I'm eleven, by the way. Isn't that unfair? Okay, I really don't want her boyfriend. It's Lukas, and he's got the thickest glasses I have ever seen on a boy. He also has this curly hair that sticks out in every direction. No, I'd much rather have someone with short hair like Jørgen. Yes, he's cute. So, please, let me have a boyfriend like that.

Dear Father Christmas,

I didn't get a boyfriend last year. And Sanne already had three. Well, actually just two. She broke up with Kevin, but now she is back with Lukas. He still has got this strange hair, so I really don't see why she likes him. I asked her, but she got mad and told me that she doesn't want to see me anymore and that I don't have a clue anyway because I never had a boyfriend. Well, if you could just give me one this year, I promise not to make fun of my sister's haircut, even if she looks like grandma Lisbeth. Sanne can keep her Lukas. He's weird, anyway. I want someone with dark hair and blue eyes like Emil. Someone to make me a cup of tea like Papa does for Mama.

Dear Father Christmas,

It's Christmas again. I finally had my first boyfriend. I'm thirteen now. So, it's past time, I think. His name is Hans. He plays soccer. I went to a Christmas luncheon at his parents' place. His mother doesn't like me. She thinks we are too young to date. His father was nice, though. He kept on telling me tales about Christmas as if I was a little girl. Hans was bored, but to be honest, I liked it. I wished that my perfect boyfriend likes to tell me tales of Christmas elves.

Dear Father Christmas,

My sister caught me writing to you. I told her that I was writing a wish list and she laughed at me. God, how I hate her sometimes. I caught her snooping through my stuff yesterday. She said that she didn't read any of my letters, but at dinner tonight, she told Mama that I am so desperate for a boyfriend, I invented one and that I should be checked. I was so mad, I threw a mushroom at her. I don't like the little buggers anyway. Mama grew mad, and I had to take dinner to my room. I hate them all! I called Sanne, but she was with Lukas. What a bad best friend! They have been dating for three years now, on and off. Sanne even talks about marriage. He has grown, but he is still that skinny guy with glasses and curly hair. And he is always staring at me as if he liked me or something. My future boyfriend shouldn't look at other girls.

Dear Father Christmas,

This year's Christmas I wish for someone patient. Sanne and Lukas broke up. She has been angry for weeks. I think it's a good thing. She always nagged him about doing this or doing that. He never did anything right. In the end, Lukas broke it off with her because she complained about him not having ordered the right coffee. She called him a "useless boyfriend" or something like that. He put the cup down and told her to find someone else to serve her. I think it was funny really. She truly has been a bitch to him forever. Maybe now, she'll stop telling me how I should get a proper boyfriend. I will, just as soon as

Christmas comes along, I'll make my wish. It's bound to work at some point, right?

Dear Father Christmas,

I thought I had found the perfect boyfriend. That's why I haven't written to you last year. But it wasn't so, alas. His name was Daniel, and he broke my heart, the jerk! Such a shame, he had the cutest smile. I considered letting him go all the way. Thank god I didn't because I caught him making out with Sanne at a party. I wanted to surprise him. Well, he was, surprised that is. Sanne has been such a bitch for ages, but this is the last straw. I turned my back on them to kiss Lukas just to make them mad. He was surprised but pleased, I think. Oh no, what have I done! I just wish for a boyfriend that will be true to me and love me. Daniel never did, obviously. Luckily, Lukas hasn't said anything. Sanne was spitting mad, though, which was kind of the point. When will you finally send me the perfect boyfriend? I have been waiting for so long.

Dear Father Christmas,

I want nothing more than to study abroad. My parents support me, why can't my boyfriend? Mike is so jealous and anxious about losing me. He told me so, and I think it's sweet, but I just want to see something of the world. It doesn't mean that I don't love him, and it's only for a year. He said, I have to choose either him or my education. My sister told me to blow him off. "If he doesn't support you, then good riddance, sis. Anyway, you won't want to study abroad with a boyfriend at home. You'll miss all the fun." I guess she's right. But once again, I'm heartbroken.

Dear Father Christmas,

I have been wishing for the perfect boyfriend for many years. This year, I only wish for you to take away my sorrows. Take them away, so that I won't have to think or feel, anymore. Mama has cancer. We found out a month ago. She is going to chemo. Her lovely chocolate hair that looks like mine has all fallen out. I watched Papa cry for the first time that I can remember. He's heartbroken, too. We all are. I'm home for Christmas. The semester is not quite over, but I don't know how I will be able to enjoy studying so far away with the burden of knowing my Mama could be dying, could actually be dead while I'm on some kind of party. As it happened, my sister called me when I was preparing for a night of bar hopping. Everything is fucked up. I wished there was someone, someone that could hold me like Papa is holding Mama when she feels down after chemo. I wish for a miracle. If you cure Mama, I will never wish for anything, no boys, no hearts, no butterflies, no tea, no one else, nothing. Please ...

Chapter 1

Roskilde

An obnoxious ringing woke me from an alcohol-induced stupor. I was just lying on the couch thinking about how I'm getting too old to meet with friends to celebrate Christmas early. The glögg really knocked me out. "I'll never drink mulled wine again!" my inner voice groaned. The ringing stopped. Sighing, I lay my head back onto the soft sofa cushions from which I had managed to partially lift it. Alas, the respite was short and not as sweet as I would have wished. The ringing might have stopped but it was replaced by a hammering sound at the door. Through the fog of my barely conscious mind, I recognised it as knocking, even though my head tried to convince me that someone was using a hammer to split it open.

I groaned, "Away, evil spirit. Get you gone!"

An evil chuckle floated through the thin door.

"I have a key, and I am not afraid to use it!" the personified evil called through the keyhole.

I groaned and turned my head ignoring the threat. As I was drifting off, the voice came again,

"Gitte?"

"I'm indisposed."

"So, I figured. But I came to drive out the demons of alcoholic over-indulgence and take you Christmas shopping."

"Bad sister!"

"She doesn't mean it, Ditte, you are a very, very good sister getting up early and taking the train all the way from Valby to make sure your baby sister has a present."

"Stop talking to yourself!"

"I'm not, right now I'm talking to a door or rather someone behind a door. For all I know, it could be the ghost of my little sis. It certainly doesn't sound very alive."

"I'm going back to sleep."

A sigh drifted through the closed door. Then my ear pricked at the sound of a key being turned. The door opened with the creak like from a bad horror movie and shut unnecessarily loud.

"Good morning!" My sadistic sister intoned like a soprano singer. I fumbled for the pillow beneath my head and threw it at her. At least, I intended to throw it, but I over-estimated my strength. In the end, I just pushed the pillow from the couch, and unfortunately out of my reach. No missile. No comfy cushion. I sighed the sigh of the sorely tested.

At least, Ditte wasn't trying to force me into an upright position, yet. Her perversely cheerful voice travelled into the kitchen. My eyes closed again. Despite the sounds of destructions from my kitchen, I managed to fall asleep again. I even dreamt. Ditte was sitting on my head happily knocking pots against each other while humming "In the Hall of the Mountain King". I woke with a start to find that I hadn't been dreaming. No, she wasn't sitting on my head, and she didn't misuse my pots. But she was humming "In the Hall of the Mountain King" while drumming a rhythm with two of my spoons.

I glared at her. She grinned back. What saved her life, in the end, was the smell wafting over from the sofa table.

"Cocoa!" my foggy mind registered with growing interest. I might have started to drool, too.

"You smell correctly," smirked Ditte.

The sadistic witch had placed the sweet ambrosia just out of my reach. With a large effort, I let my cadaver roll to the floor. Step two was to push my butt close enough to the small table so that I could let my tongue sink into the heavenly hot chocolate. The concentration must have been obvious on my face because, with an exasperated laugh, Ditte took the mug and pushed it into my largely lifeless hands. I took a sip.

"That's how Mary must have felt on Christmas Day!" I exclaimed passionately.

"You think my hot chocolate is as good as the birth of the son of God?" She paused, made a thoughtful face, then lit up like a Christmas tree, "It's surely divine if I say so myself."

I wasn't listening any more. As long as my mug was full, my mind was preoccupied, and the day hadn't started, yet.

Like always when my cocoa threatened to disappear, I looked sadly upon the last sip. Before I could start to whine, however, Ditte ripped the mug out of my hands, drained the last drop, and looked at me challengingly.

"Evil sister!" I moaned.

"I simply cannot take your puppy face, little sis. Now go and take a shower, and for heaven's sake, brush your teeth ... twice."

I didn't bother to argue. My headache was reduced to a simmer, and there was no getting out of arrangements with Ditte. So, I crawled to the bathroom and did as I was told.

Stepping out of the shower, I felt almost normal again. A pile of fresh clothes lay on the toilet seat. Ditte must have laid it out for me. I hurried to put it on with displeasure. If I didn't hurry, she would probably tidy up my flat, too.

Sure enough, my dirty clothes from the night before were nowhere to be seen. Neither were the shoes I must have dropped somewhere. I couldn't remember where. God, that had been a good glögg! The cushions were back on the couch, even the one I have been looking for in weeks, dirty dishes were being washed by the sound of it, and an open window blew freezing air into my admittedly thick-aired flat. All in all, everything was neater than it had been in ages, and I couldn't find my shoes.

"Hey, Ditte, where are my shoes, praise your housewifely arse?"

"Let me think," an ironic voice replied. "I found one on the stairs on my way up and the other in front of your neighbour's door."

"How do you know they were mine?"

"Who else wears Father Christmas boots?"

I smiled. They were red with a white fur lining and small golden stars. I loved those boots.

"If someone had tripped over them," Ditte continued clearly striving to dampen my blossoming good moods. "Everybody would have known who to blame."

"Damn!" In my drunken stupor, I must have thought the whole building my domain. Thank God, nobody had tripped. I thought about the sweet elderly Lone from next door. She had baked Christmas cookies just for me. The thought made my face muscles relax. I strolled resolutely to the cupboard and took out a few of Lone's cookies.

"Hey, I made you a sandwich"! cried Ditte.

"Uuh!" I cooed. "That goes perfectly with my biscuits."

I snatched the plate out of Ditte's hand and gobbled everything down.

"You look like a snake. Don't forget to chew. Sometimes, I question your influence on my daughter."

"Hey," I wanted to cry in outrage, but my mouth was full. So, it came out more like "eeeeym!"

"Since you won't even take the time to sit much less chew, I suggest we go shopping now," Ditte said. "Tobias will be around with Bitte at 1 PM."

I nodded, swallowed the last bite of my sandwich, and went on a hunt for my shoes. Bitte's father was always punctual and practical to a fault. He and Ditte had been best friends since high school. All the more unusual the two of them decided to have a short affair resulting in the loveliest little girl I had ever seen. They didn't stay together, though.

"No sizzle," Ditte used to tell everybody. To me, she confessed that she didn't think Tobias had it in him to be in a relationship and be a real father. He took care of Bitte, but he was more like an uncle to her than a parent.

The morning was spent Christmas shopping at the pedestrian street Algade in my hometown Roskilde, where I still lived in a small flat not far from the harbour. I bought gifts for myself, my father, and Bitte. I couldn't very well buy a gift for Ditte with her present. My father would be getting a nice pair of woolly socks, red of course, with a cheery looking elf printed on each one. I bought some for me, too. Ditte eyed my choice sceptically and bought a crossword puzzle. As far as Christmas gifts went, we obviously had very different tastes. For Bitte, I got a snow globe with two elves ice skating on a frozen lake. There were really a lot of elves or nisser to be had in Roskilde at this time of year. I loved it!

At precisely 1 PM, we met Tobias at Roskilde station. Bitte was all dressed up with boots, winter jacket, mittens, a shawl, and cab. She moved with difficulty. I smiled.

"Gitte!" she cried enthusiastically.

"Bitte!" I shouted back falling on my knees and hugging the six-year-old as if I hadn't seen her in years, even though I saw her almost every week.

We ate lunch at a café. Afterwards, Tobias left for the station. Ditte and Bitte went home with me to get the imp settled. She would stay with me tonight so that her mother could have time to meet up with a guy she liked. It must be serious. This was the third or so date. She didn't say much about it, though.

"I don't want to introduce just any man into my daughter's life."

I got that she didn't talk about him to Bitte, but what about me?

"You're almost like my second daughter, little sis," Ditte would say laughing her head off.

I scowled.

After Ditte left, Bitte and I watched a Christmas programme for a while drinking cocoa with cinnamon. It was so cosy, I almost fell asleep. That was until Bitte jumped up and exclaimed, "I want to go to the fjord!"

I looked bleary-eyed out of the window.

"In this weather?" I pleaded. It was still light outside, but the wind was ruffling the tree branches in front of the house whirling yellow leaves against the glass. I shivered just thinking about it.

"Of course," Bitte replied imperiously.

"But it is surely very cold," I threatened.

"It won't be," she huffed.

"Don't force me," I whined.

"Maybe there's snow," she tempted.

I considered first her sly face, then the grey clouds outside.

"Maybe," I said hesitantly.

That was enough to get Bitte going. She ran back and forth picking up my boots – one of them at least – my shawl and mittens.

"Where's my coat?" I asked.

"Couldn't find it, of course."

It was my time to huff. I only had to look for it for ten minutes finally detecting it on a chair beneath a tartan patterned blanket. I slipped it on, then helped Bitte with her clothes. She had to tell me that I had forgotten my mittens, but I remembered every item of her clothes.

When I was sure that we hadn't forgotten to put on anything else, I grabbed my bag and my niece, and off we were.

Roskilde is located on the South end of a long fjord. To get to the water, we needed to go through the city park Byparken until we reached the harbour. An ugly square building housed the Viking Ship Museum. I hadn't been there in ages. Never since Mama fell ill.

"Maybe I should", I mused as we passed it by. We crossed a bridge and took a path that let along the harbour and the fjord. One could walk for hours without ever reaching the sea. Bitte's legs were too short to walk far and it was soon getting dark anyway. So, we went to our favourite spot, a little sandy beach not far from the harbour. Ducks and seagulls shouted at each other in the distance. Bitte immediately ran towards the water to test how cold it was. She cried out shaking her hand. I kneeled down, following her example.

"It's so cold!" we yelled in unison while laughing and shaking our burning hands.

"Look!" Bitte suddenly said, her voice full of awe.

Her gaze was fixed on a point to the left. Someone was standing in the ice-cold water. A closer look revealed a man. He wore a jacket; his jeans were rolled up above his knees. From this angle, I could see his profile. He had a prominent chin and a straight nose. His blond hair was wind-blown and looked much like a halo in the stream of sunlight that peeked out of the clouds for just a second. I might have classified him as sexy were it not for his legs being submerged in freezing water. This made me rather tend towards crazy instead.

Speaking about crazy, I just managed to grab for my equally afflicted niece. While I had been ogling the sexy madman, Bitte had taken off her shoes and socks. She was in the process of stepping into the water when I caught hold of her. She looked at me innocently.

"What?"

"Are you planning to copy that?" my chin pointed at Sexy Madman.

"Of course," she replied without a care in the world.

"Your mother would kill me."

"You should try it, too."

"So? I just put my hand in the water and nearly lost my fingers, and you think I would put my feet into the stuff?"

"Of course."

I groaned. She was right. I would. So, I took off my shoes and socks pouting all the while. When I was ready, we took each other by the hand. I counted to three.

We squealed in terror when the burning water touched our skin. Just as fast as she was in Bitte jumped out. My squeal turned into an awkward shout as Bitte's fast retreat led to me falling backwards into the wet sand.

"Bitte!" I yelped in outrage.

My jeans were wet up to my waist. For a while, I just sat there in shock with my legs still partially submerged in cold water. Then I had the presence of mind to crawl backwards. Bitte appeared next to me. She looked half shame-faced, half amused.

"Sorry, it was really cold," she tried to excuse her fast retreat.

I glared at her, "Who is supposed to be the adult here?"

"Me?"

"Exactly, now let's go home."

I didn't cherish a twenty minutes' walk in my wet jeans. Too bad I didn't think of bringing towels to dry off. Who is supposed to be the adult, indeed? I should have known that visiting the fjord with Bitte would end in wet clothes.

"Excuse me."

I looked up from my undignified sitting position to find Sexy Madman towering over me. He looked like a giant, at least from my vantage point. His voice sounded deep and strangely raspy as if he had difficulties forcing the words out. A short perusal of his face revealed high cheekbones, a straight nose, and a square chin covered with beard stubble. I was right before. He was sexy. I couldn't make out the colour of his eyes. It was too dark already. What I did notice was that they were not quite meeting mine. His hair stuck out in all directions. They quite reminded me of someone.

"Hi there, nice day for a swim!" I said cheerfully. Under my breath, I added, "When you're a polar bear."

"Let me help you up," he said as if I hadn't said anything.

I took the offered hand. It was large in my own. A rush of excitement pumped through my veins. So, I forgot to let go when I stood on my own feet. He was tall, more than a head taller than me, and I wasn't short. The faintest hint of red coloured his cheeks.

"Gitte, there's a lot of sand on your butt," Bitte interrupted my perusal of Sexy Madman.

Despite his obvious discomfort, he hadn't made a move to reclaim his hand. I let go immediately embarrassed that I had held it for so long. I glared at Bitte, but she only had eyes for the man in front of us.

"Why were you standing in the water?" she asked.

He smiled down to her, his face almost relieved. His voice as he answered had lost some of its hoarseness as well, "I like looking out at the fjord and feeling the water surrounding me."

"But it's so cold," Bitte cried shaking herself.

"Yes, but I like the bite."

Bitte beamed adoringly up at him. He smiled kindly back. However, the talk of cold water had reminded me of something.

"Speaking of cold water, I should get us home before we catch a cold."

"Right," he said and turned red again. "You can borrow my towel to dry off."

He retrieved a large towel from a pile of clothing I hadn't noticed before and held it out to me. I took it. First, I used it to dry Bitte. When her clothes were back on, I dried my own feet, tried unsuccessfully to get rid of the sand stuck to my butt, and finally handed the towel back. I was starting to feel truly cold now. The wind was always fierce down here, and my clothes were wet.

"You can borrow this," he fumbled for another towel and handed it to me.

"Don't you need it to dry off yourself?" I asked hesitating to make someone else freeze just because he wanted to be nice.

"I'll just take the other towel."

"Why do you have two?" Bitte chimed in.

There was the smile again, "I was thinking about going all the way in, but the water really is too shallow here."

"All the way?" Bitte said in awe.

"Anyway," I interrupted with a warning look in Bitte's direction because I was so cold by now that I didn't care about being rude. "You're sure I may borrow the towel?"

"Sure."

I wrapped it around my waist, which helped marginally against the cold. If it hadn't been for the obvious discomfort of the stranger, I would have taken my wet jeans off. As it was, I feared his instant combustion.

"So, gorgeous," I attempted a flirty tone. "What's your name, and how can I reach you to return your kindness?"

I was talking about returning the towel. This time, his cheeks almost lit up the falling darkness as if I had made an improper proposal. I almost giggled at the thought.

"It's Lukas. I'm a shipwright at the museum." He pointed to where the Viking Ship Museum could have been seen, were it not for the Trees that obscured the view. Something else struck me, though. I looked at his wind-blown hair again, and then it came to me.

"Lukas? Lukas Holm Eriksen?" I asked.

He nodded. I squealed for the second time and threw my arms around his neck. Surprised by my outburst, he put his hands on my waist to steady me.

"I haven't seen you in ages!" I exclaimed. "How are you? Oh, you don't know who I am, right?"

My hands were still intertwined behind his neck. Our faces were just a breath apart, and for the first time, his eyes met mine. They looked almost black in the oncoming darkness.

"Yes, I know who you are, Gitte. It's been a long time."

Chapter 2

Shortly after our chance meeting with Lukas, it had started to snow, which had delighted Bitte but reminded me of how good a warm bath would be. We had excused ourselves. I resisted the urge to look back when we arrived at the harbour. Snowflakes started to cover the earth in a thin layer of white. The fjord lay still and mystical. A strange feeling of something lying in the air took hold of me. I wasn't sure if I wanted to find out, yet. So, I turned my back on the sight for now.

I was still mulling over the encounter with Lukas when Bitte and I returned to my flat. It must have been nearly nine years since I saw him last. He did turn out to be a handsome devil after all. Who would have thought?

Bitte was smitten. She went on and on about wanting to go to the Viking Ship Museum to see Lukas again. I wasn't sure whether I truly wanted to renew our acquaintance. He seemed embarrassed at best to meet me. I thought about us ogling him, me wet and covered in sand, me throwing my arms around him. Why must I always be so impulsive? When Ditte came to pick up her daughter, Bitte chatted on excitedly about our encounter trying her best to persuade her mother to take her to the museum. Ditte agreed readily and with a little blush. She didn't even give me a hard time about endangering Bitte with cold water. I was too much in my own head to have an argument anyway, much less ask her about her date. By the time I thought about it, the two of them were long gone. I tried to call her later in the evening but she didn't pick up the phone. I frowned. How often did I tell her to pick up the phone, else I worry until I reach her?

Instead, I called Papa. At least he always took his calls right away.

"Lars speaking," he grumbled into the phone.

"Good evening to you, Lars. I got you a nice Christmas present."

He groaned, "Nothing can top the boxer briefs from last year."

"Didn't they fit?"

"They had bumble bees printed on them."

"You said you liked bumblebees."

"In my garden, not on my underwear, sweetheart."

"Well, I promise, no bumblebees this year."

"I will like anything you get me."

"That's a very noble attitude. How is Julie?"

Papa had had a girlfriend for four years now. I was glad that he wasn't alone. However, I don't deny that it was weird in the beginning, and Ditte spent a lot of time persuading me to give her a chance, even though I already had every intention of doing so. It wasn't difficult, either. Julie was a darling. When I found out about her proclivity for baking, I was totally hooked. She had three children, Alan, Asger, and Anna. Yes, it was odd that all their names started with A. However, Ditte pointed out the names our gracious parents had gifted us with, and I really couldn't argue about that.

I chatted with Papa for a while. We usually talked about two or three times a week, and I visited him once a week, at least. Sometimes, I felt as if I was intruding on his life. He never complained, though.

"I love you to bits, old man," I said impulsively.

"I love you, too, sweetheart," he replied without missing a beat. He was used to my outbursts of affection. There was a pause. Everything had been said. I knew that Papa was waiting for me to end the call. He never did. I wondered if he realised how much I appreciated this. We said our goodbyes.

Later in bed, I thought about my small family. I liked to keep them all close. It bothered me that Ditte lived in Valby, which was more than twenty minutes with the train from Roskilde station. Then again, if she still lived in Roskilde, I'd probably be at her place every day. She couldn't handle that much love, surely. I smiled to myself, but the smile was faltering a little. Maybe I was too clingy. This is why I hadn't had a man in my life for more than a few months and not any in more than two years. I knew it was all right to cling to my family. A guy would be less understanding. Not that I ever tried that theory. The thought of letting someone else into my life, whom I could lose, scared the hell out of me.

Involuntarily my thoughts conjured an image of a tall bare-footed Viking, his blond curls ruffled by the wind, his shy dark eyes never meeting mine. That was unexpected. I remembered Lukas as this nerdy boy. He had never said much, even then, always hanging around the harbour or with Sanne. The thought of my former best friend made my blood curdle even after all those years. She had been fun to be with because of her mischievous mind. Since I wasn't an angel myself, we had fit perfectly. On the other hand, she kept on ordering people about. I had still clung to our friendship until my mother had fallen ill. She had turned out to care little about my desperation. It wasn't hard to let her go back then. I wondered if Lukas was still seeing her.

Shaking my head, I punched my pillow and tried to put myself to sleep. It was no use. The image of Lukas stayed with me throughout the night and the next days. He even followed me to work.

"Gitte! Gitte!"

My mind slowly returned to the present. I looked at a class of expats who wanted to learn Danish. Twelve very different faces looked back at me, an Afghan, two Germans, an Indian, an Indonesian, two Italians, three Chinese girls, a Polish guy, and two Spaniards.

"Excuse me, I was in my own head," I said cheerfully. "What was your question, Abdulla?"

The Afghan smiled indulgently back at me, "I was just wondering; how do you say in Danish, I would like some of this hot spiced wine they sell at the market?"

"You say, Jeg vil gerne have et glas glögg. It goes really well with æbleskiver I might add. They are like pancakes."

I wrote the words on the whiteboard.

"Maybe we should go to an exhibition at the market. To improve our language skills, of course," Jorge, one of the Spaniards chimed in casting a wicked smile in my direction.

"Afraid a field trip isn't in my schedule," I answered regretfully. Then again, thinking back to my glögg escapade from last Friday, maybe I wasn't that regretful after all. "However, you guys should go and practise together. There's a nice market at Stændertorv by the city hall. Check it out and tell me what you ordered next week. Remember, Jeg vil gerne have et glas glögg eller to eller tre. The more the better, actually."

On that cheery note, I dismissed them to prepare for the module three examination. There were five modules, six if you wanted to study at the university in Danish. Usually, it took most of the expats less than a year to learn the language. After three months, most of them were confident enough to have small conversations of which they reported back to me enthusiastically. I envied them somewhat. I lived the excitement of studying abroad for all of a little over a year until it all turned rotten.

"Don't think about it," I murmured to myself.

"What was that?" a voice with a distinct Spanish accent asked next to me.

I jumped and let my papers fly. Luckily, Jorge managed to catch the lot of them never losing his smile in the process.

"Jorge! Don't sneak up on me like that!" I cried theatrically grasping my heart. "It makes me scream, and then I might lose my voice, and then I can't teach, and then I might lose my job, and then I'd have to live with my sister, and then I would kill her for stealing my biscuits. She always does that, the witch!"

Jorge's laugh interrupted my stream of consciousness.

"You are really funny, Gitte," he smiled. "I would like to go out with you sometime. Would you like to go to the Christmas market with me?"

I stared at him in puzzlement, unsure of how we came to this point.

"Ah," I sighed. "Don't tell anyone, but I actually don't like glögg and æbleskiver. Still, as a Dane, it is expected of you to sell the national goods of your countries to foreigners, nonetheless."

"I see," he said not believing a word of what I said. "Maybe another time, another place. Hav en god dag, Gitte!"

"I lige måde. Likewise," I replied watching him go.

He had a nice broad back. I gave him that. Yet, like Ditte always used to say, "No sizzle."

Chapter 3

I left school at 8 PM. The weather was freezing cold, and as usual, I had forgotten my mittens. Sometimes I thought about sowing them together with a string like Bitte's were. She never forgot her mittens.

"Don't be too hard on yourself," I gave myself credit. "You don't have a mother to check that you're wearing them, any longer."

The thought didn't cheer me up. Neither did riding my bike home through the slippery streets. Snow had fallen in the weekend. By Monday, every single flake had melted to an unappetising mass on the roads. Even though my hands were threatening to freeze off, I took the longer route home. I rode down the pedestrian street with all the Christmas lights cheering me up. The shops were closed, but I stopped at Stændertorv to sit at a café.

While I sipped my coffee, I tried calling Ditte again. This time I was lucky. She answered at the third ring.

"Hi little sis," Ditte said over-cheerfully, a tone she adopted whenever she felt bad about not answering the phone.

"Hey, how goes?"

"Well enough, we just made some biscuits and confections. I suspect that the confections will be vanished by tomorrow. I could bring myself to hide some biscuits for you, though."

"Ginger nuts?"

"Of course."

I whooped delightedly, "Yes, yes, yes!"

"You're worse than Bitte," Ditte laughed. "Why don't you learn to bake if you like to eat so much?"

"Weight control among other things."

"Right," Ditte drawled. "Where are you anyway?"

"At a café."

"With whom?"

"My pleasant self. But wait, how was your date?"

"Oh right," she said trying and failing to sound as if she wasn't dying to tell. "It was great."

"Tell me sis, or you are not allowed to bake for me ever again."

"What kind of threat is that? All right, his name is Bo. He lives in Roskilde and has a little daughter around Bitte's age. And he's cute and funny and has a personality. You know how many people just seem to be weird?"

"You mean like talking about former girlfriends, their obsession with collecting trains, wearing dresses, or even worse going on and on about their fantastic relationship with their mother?"

"Precisely, and that's just the first date. Well, he only has his father and a cousin he is very close to apparently. We went to Tivoli. I hadn't been on a roller coaster in years. You know, I was wearing this short skirt, and he just picked me up and turned me around and around until I was dizzy, and then we kissed. He is such a good kisser, too."

"Oh, I love amusement parks! But wait, you rode on a rollercoaster?"

"Yeah, so what?"

"So, is he deaf now."

"Ha-ha, I didn't scream."

"No?"

"Well, not that much."

"My hearing is still impacted by you screaming into my ears as a child."

"That's just an excuse for ignoring my sound advice."

We kept on bickering for a while, until my coffee was cold. It was time to go.

"I better get home, now," I said.

"Oh wait, I forgot, I'm planning to introduce Bo to Bitte during the weekend. We're going to visit him at work."

"Wow, that's a big step."

"Yeah, I know. So, I thought you'd lighten the pressure on all of us if you tagged along."

"All right, where does he work?"

"At the Viking Ship Museum."

My thoughts immediately travelled to last Saturday when I had met Lukas. He said he was working at the museum, too.

"Gitte, are you still there?"

"Yes, of course, I will come."

A strange mixture of excitement and foreboding pressed down on me. I was looking forward to maybe seeing Lukas again. On the other hand, I felt strange thinking about how good-looking he was compared to when we went to school. I was wondering how he had turned out. Obviously, he was gorgeous. But there was this strange shyness or maybe he was just not happy to see me. That wouldn't be surprising given that I never made a secret of not liking him very much when he was with Sanne.

"Oh, thank you," Ditte interrupted my musing. "Bo promised to show us the workshop where they are building the ships. Too bad we can't go on a trip with the Viking ships, now."

"We should definitely do that in the summer. I can't even remember the last time I tried that."

"I can."

"Figures."

"Yes, I was so wet from your fidgeting. I believe they would have prohibited you from ever stepping a foot on the Viking ships again if I hadn't been such a cute sweetheart."

I snorted, "Yeah, keep telling yourself that. However, let me just point out who dripped ice-cream on a poor woman's coat."

"It was a fur coat!" she cried in outrage. "Poor animals had to die for that coat."

"I'm with you. The bitch deserved nothing less. Still, Papa had to endure her shrieking. That might have been the only time I heard Mama yell at a stranger. It was fantastic."

"Yeah," Ditte agreed.

We decided to meet on Saturday around 1 PM at my place. I hung up the phone, drained the cold liquid in my cup with a regretful last glance, and put on my coat. Before I could leave, I was called back. A waitress handed me my cap with an indulgent smile. I sighed and took it. So that's how I kept on losing all my stuff.

Chapter 4

The week flew by in a rush. I always tried to cherish the advent by frequenting Christmas markets despite what I told Jorge. So, I met with friends to go Christmas shopping in Copenhagen. There was a nice market at Østregasværk with hand-made soaps. I loved soaps. Every year, I bought some and hid them like Easter eggs around my flat. I found them in my clothes, my shoes, my pots even in the microwave. That was a mess to clean up. I might have left a bit for Ditte to enjoy. Between this trip, calling Papa, Ditte, teaching at the language school, and generally doing my best to get into the Christmas mood by playing seasonal music,

Saturday came too early for my liking.

This time, I managed to get up before Ditte's unceremonious wake-up call. So, when the doorbell rang, I had the cocoa prepared for a second breakfast. I opened the door and held my hand out. Ditte knew what I wanted. She still ignored my rude gesture.

"Gitte!" Bitte threw her arms around my waist. I hugged her back. Then, I turned her around for a threatening gesture.

"Give me my ginger nuts if you ever want to see your daughter again."

"Keep her, she never makes her bed in the morning," Ditte replied with a shrug.

"Mama!" Bitte wailed.

Her mother turned around, "Just kidding."

I squeezed her small body. Maybe she was too young to understand our jokes sometimes. Reassured, Bitte grinned up to me.

"We're going to see how they build the ships like true Vikings."

"We sure are," I winked. "But first things first."

I darted for Ditte's bag.

"Hey!" Ditte shouted.

Too late. I triumphantly held up the paper-wrapped goodies.

"Just what a girl needs."

Ditte groaned, "Only two. We're going to eat lunch later."

"Ok," Bitte and I agreed in unison.

We devoured the cocoa and ginger nuts in no time. As always, Ditte finished hers last, leaving Bitte and me to cast rueful glances at her half-full cocoa mug. She didn't let herself be deterred by our behaviour. She never had. I exchanged a speculative glance with Bitte. When Ditte took a sip of her cocoa, I grabbed the last of her ginger nut, broke it in half, and tossed one to Bitte.

Ditte made a show of scowling at us, "What are you teaching my daughter?"

"Nothing's forbidden when it comes to ginger nuts?" I asked with a full mouth.

"You mean in love and war?"

"That too."

We all laughed.

A crisp wind blew around our noses as we made our way down to the museum. Bitte held both of our hands and chatted on and on about ships. I was wondering about the sudden interest until she asked, "Can we go to the fjord and swim later?"

"We can go to the fjord but no swimming. It's too cold."

"But Lukas did," Bitte pouted.

"He was just in with his feet. You already tried that."

"Yes."

"And wasn't it cold?"

"Yes, but I want to try again."

"At first, we'll go to the museum. Later, we'll see," Ditte amended, knowing full well that the chance of Bitte forgetting everything by the end of the day was good.

"Very well," Bitte agreed imperiously.

I loved that kid.

The museum truly wasn't much to look at. A square concrete building, it somewhat stood out from the otherwise beautiful fjord and harbour. The only one who looked at it in excitement was Bitte. We let go of her hands and off she was inspecting the anchored ships. We didn't have the heart to tell her that the motor boats she was marvelling over couldn't exactly be called Viking ships.

At the entrance, we were met by a dark-haired guy with matching eyes and a big smile. He was huge much like Lukas. Judging by the way he immediately strolled towards us, I imagined him to be Bo. He stopped in front of us giving Bitte a smile before enveloping her mother in a bear hug. For a second there, I was worried about crushed bones.

Bitte looked at me in surprise. Clearly, she had never seen Ditte hugged by a guy before. Probably because the only man in her life so far had been Tobias, and he wasn't the hugging type. He rarely bestowed one on his own daughter. When the hug didn't seem to end, I tried to discreetly clear my throat. They sprang apart as if I had blown into a trumpet, their ears turning red.

"I hope you're Bo. Otherwise, this would be awkward," I jested.

"Oh, yes, sorry," he said flustered sticking out his hand. There was something familiar about his blushed face. He looked a lot like someone else who was supposed to be working here. My eyes roamed the entrance. There was no sign of Lukas.

We all looked at Bitte to observe her reaction. Ditte bent down to talk to her daughter.

"Sweetie, this is Bo. He'll show us around. You'll get to see the ships you were so excited about. Is that all right?"

Bitte nodded clearly unsure of herself.

"You know, I have a daughter at your age. Alexa," Bo said in a soft baritone. "Do you know what she likes best about the museum?"

"What?" Bitte said hesitantly.

"The costumes," he chuckled.

"What kind of costumes?"

"Well," Bo said, "you can try on clothes worn by Vikings over a thousand years ago."

Bitte didn't answer, but her face lit up in excitement.

"Do they have some for adults, too?" I enthused in her stead.

"You can try and see if they fit," Bo said failing to conceal his amusement.

"As you see, I have two children to entertain today. I hope you don't mind."

"He won't," I chimed in waving her off. "We're too lovable, right Bitte?"

"Of course," the imp agreed in her usual arrogance.

"Cool, let me just have a look at the vicinities first," I said.

Bo looked nonplussed.

"The toilets are over there," Ditte sighed.

After relieving my pea-sized bladder, we started inspecting the exhibition. Five Viking ships in different states of decay had been found in the Roskilde fjord. They had been used to barricade the fjord from enemy ships. For hundreds of years, they were submerged in water. The Viking Ship Museum was built for the purpose of restoring and conserving their remains for the future.

I couldn't help but look at the ships with nostalgia. The last time I had seen them, Ditte and I were still children. Mama had been in love with everything Viking-related, attending talks about the building of Viking ships, raids, ship burials and such whenever she could. Every year, we had taken a tour around Roskilde fjord on one of the tourist boats.

Absently, I followed the others through the main hall of the museum. Bitte listened excitedly to Bo's explanations of open water battles. He was a good storyteller keeping it simple. The best part, of course, was the dressing up. Bitte and I dove into the small stack of clothes. I growled at a girl trying to take the dress I wanted. It was red, shapeless, and sleeveless. A kind of fur cloak was thrown around the shoulders. I took a selfie of me and Bitte.

An older lady in the corner was weaving a grey piece of wool. When we approached, she lifted her head and smiled up at Bo.

"Hey Mary, could you tell us a little bit about your work here?"

The older woman nodded invitingly. She was weaving parts of a sail that would be sewn together later.

"How long until it's finished?" Bitte asked.

"About three years," Mary answered.

"Wow, so long?"

"Yes, the sail is the most important part of the ship. It takes a long time to make and is very expensive. There's a story about a ship's captain. He was a very proud Viking warrior. His ship was one of the largest of them all, and he never came back from a raid without gain. But when his sail was destroyed in a storm, he wept like a child."

"That's stupid, why cry over a sail?" Bitte giggled.

"You'd cry if your teddy was destroyed, wouldn't you?" asked Ditte.

Bitte pondered the question for a while: before finally admitting, "Maybe I would."

Mary showed Bitte the loom she was working on, explained a little about how the two sets of threads had to be interlaced, and let her touch the ruff fabric of the sail.

More knowledgeable in the arts of weaving and shipbuilding, we said our goodbyes. Ditte opted for eating lunch at the café. I checked and found myself not too full to eat another sandwich or two.

"So, what did you like best?" Bo asked Bitte.

"The costumes!" she said without missing a beat.

"I'm not surprised," he laughed. "You remind me a lot of Alexa."

"Oh no, so bad, ha?" I teased.

Bitte gave me the glare of death.

"Just a joke?" I said trying for a subdued tone.

She only sniffed with contempt.

"I thought I could show you our workshop after lunch. We restore old Viking ships and make replicas."

"What's a replica?" Bitte asked, her wrath against me forgotten.

"We try to build Viking ships just as they used to look like," Bo said.

"Oh, do you sail them, too?" Bitte said with barely contained excitement.

"Sure," Bo said. "Not in winter, though. It's too cold to sail. We usually take them out of the water in November. The low temperature isn't good for the wood. In April we repaint them, and as soon as it gets warmer, we take them out to sail. Sometimes the boat guild takes longer trips. We have been to Berlin and even Dublin a few years back."

"May I go?" Bitte immediately begged.

"Maybe in the summer," Ditte asked again counting on her daughter's bad memory.

"So, would you like to see our workshop?" Bo reminded Bitte of his previous question.

"Oh yes," she said.

The Viking ship harbour was located between the museum and the rest of the harbour. Bo led us to a large wooden building.

"We're working outside in the summer. You can come and visit us and see how everything is fitted together. Today, it's pretty closed up."

It was already getting dark. A few Christmas lights were lit around the shape of a big ship lying upside down on the shore.

"That's Havhingsten, the Sea Stallion," Bo explained.

We entered the workshop. Inside, everything smelled of wood. I took a deep breath. At a table, a man was bending over something we couldn't see from our perspective. He was so immersed in what he was mulling over that he hadn't noticed our approach, yet. Bo cast us an exasperated glance before slapping his hand on his colleague's back. The sound echoed through the largely silent building. To my astonishment, the mistreated didn't move a muscle. I would have been half-way to the moon had someone snuck up on me in that way.

The man just rolled his shoulders as if nothing happened, righted himself, and said, "Bo, the nail isn't right. See?"

His voice was deep and just a little bit hoarse. I would have recognised it anywhere. I barely registered the wooden nail he was holding up without even looking over his shoulder.

"Lukas, we have company," said Bo rolling his eyes.

Slowly, he turned around. His eyebrows were raised, at least while he was taking in Bo and Ditte. When his gaze travelled over Bitte and me, his brows dropped accompanied by his eyes. His cheeks turned red.

"This is Ditte," Bo made the introductions. "This is her daughter Bitte. She's a blast."

Bitte beamed at Bo. He truly seemed to be the charmer I had believed him to be. "And that's Gitte, her sister."

"Nice to meet you," Lukas said shaking himself and then our hands.

"We've met before," cried Bitte.

"I remember," he smiled down at her, his voice slightly less hoarse. "The little lady pushing her auntie into the cold fjord, right?"

"I didn't push her," she protested.

"You're telling me she jumped on her own?" he asked.

"Of course," Bitte replied.

"What a foolish thing to do," Lukas exclaimed.

"Yeah," answered the little traitor.

"Hey!" I protested.

Lukas stopped joking with Bitte at once. His eyes shortly met mine before flickering away.

"I thought I'd show them around our workshop, explain a bit about the ships and how they are built. Does that bother you?"

Lukas shook his head, "Go on, but watch out for the little lady, less she sails off with one of our ships."

He winked at Bitte, who looked adoringly back up at him. That was a girl in love if ever I saw one.

"Are you coming, Gitte?" Ditte asked when I didn't follow them right away.

I had had quite enough of ships at this point.

"I'll just hang around with Lukas for a little while if that's all right with you."

The others shrugged and moved on leaving an awkward silence behind. Lukas was still standing there obviously not knowing what to do now that the others had turned their attention to the tools on the wall. For some strange reason, he seemed to be most uncomfortable with me. I wondered why that was.

"A nice big nail you have there," I said. If possible, he became even redder. "I mean that one," I laughed pointing at the wooden nail he was still holding.

"Oh right," he rasped out in sudden understanding.

"What are you going to do with it?"

"It's faulty. I got to straighten it up a little."

"How is it faulty?"

"You see, the wood has to dry for a few months before it goes into the ship. It will change its shape a little during that time. That's why the nail needs to have the right size. I cannot adjust it afterwards. Otherwise, it won't fit the hole."

I had a wonderfully immature comeback to that but managed to hold my tongue.

"May I see it?" I asked instead. He handed me the nail. The barest brush of his skin against mine resonated through my whole body.

"Later, I will sharpen the end so that the nail doesn't splinter when it's hammered into the ship," Lukas explained.

I wasn't even looking at the nail. I was looking at his face. His stubble had grown into a small beard since I last saw him. His hair stood on end giving him the look of a lion. His eyes were something between grey and blue in the light of the surrounding lamps. There was a palpable tension between us. Even though Lukas was as red as an apple, he didn't move away.

"So, you're working together with Bo?" I asked to ease the tension.

"Yes, he's my cousin."

"I didn't know you had a cousin."

"Ah," he said uncomfortably. "We weren't friends back then. You didn't seem to like me very much when we went to school. Oh, but he didn't go to the same school, either."

"Don't worry, I'm not insulted," I tried to reassure him. "I was a witch at that time, and to be honest, I thought you were kind of a nerd."

"Still am, actually. Nothing's changed there," he gulped before rasping out, "I thought you were funny and carefree. I liked that about you."

"Well, everything's changed there," I said more bitter than I had planned.

"Um, I like the shorter hair, anyway. It suits you," he said in an effort to erase my embarrassing outburst of emotion no doubt.

"For a shy guy you are quite the charmer, Lukas Holm Eriksen," I said tugging on the dark strands hovering just above my jawline. I shot a glance at his mass of golden curls, my fingers itching to touch them. The thought made me recoil. When had I ever wanted to touch someone I just met, even if he was a gorgeous former classmate?

"I try," he said with a faint smile.

"So, how did you end up here?" I made a hand gesture that included the workshop.

"I always liked ships. Well, Bo and I did. We studied shipbuilding and were lucky enough to get an internship here."

"Do you sail the ships, too?"

"Yes, I'm a member of the boat guild that sailed the Sea Stallion to Berlin a few years ago. There was an exhibition in 2014. We rowed the ship through the whole city. Unfortunately, without a sail. All the low bridges make sailing impossible."

"I read about that. How was it?"

"It was the best. Did you see the Sea Stallion outside?"

I nodded.

"It's the Sea Stallion of Glendalough, a copy of one of the ships found in the fjord. The original is from Ireland. That's why the boat guild sailed it to Dublin in 2007, to prove that it's possible. We're sailing smaller versions of the Viking ships through the fjord in the summer but for now, the season is over."

Lukas cast a sad look at his workbench.

"I wished I could have sailed to Dublin with them," he said as if to himself. "It must have been great, sailing over open water for seven weeks."

"I've been on one of the smaller ships once. It was ages ago," I said. "I remember how hard it was to row the thing."

The comment made him laugh. The sound wasn't as raspy as I would have thought considering his perpetually hoarse

43

voice. It was a deep booming sound. My heart jumped in response.

"You need a bit of muscle, that's true."

"I can see that," I answered with an appreciative look at his biceps.

Instantly, the blush was back in his face. Intending to soothe him, my hand developed a mind of its own shooting out to squeeze his arm. The muscle flexed beneath my fingers. For the first time today, Lukas' eyes met mine full on. I couldn't read their expression. Embarrassed, I let go of his arm as if burned. That's how I felt. Burned. My cheeks were burning most of all.

"What a pair we make," I thought. "Both lit up like a Christmas tree."

"What have you been up to, Gitte?" Lukas asked his eyes wandering downwards again. "You said you have changed. In what way?"

"Did I say that," I laughed trying not to sound as nervous as I felt. "I meant nothing by it. Just that I'm a teacher at the language school now. Who would have thought that, right? Me, a teacher. But I like the work."

"I imagine you are very good at it," he said. There was more. His voice told me that he knew there was more, more I didn't say. This time, I didn't meet his eyes.

"Yeah ... well, it's a way of travelling without travelling if you know what I mean," I stuttered in a rush.

He didn't answer. I sought out his eyes. They were much closer now than they had been a minute ago. A strange expression filled them, something between curiosity and tenderness. My hand lifted of its own accord itching to touch the stubble on his jaw. I never got the chance. The voices of our relatives interrupted us. Especially Bitte's voice rang out like a bell breaking the tension that hung thickly between Lukas and me. I hadn't realised how close we were standing up until now. I expected him to draw back. I certainly had the impulse. If only my limbs weren't made of pudding. However, our approaching relatives didn't seem to deter Lukas. His own hand lifted to hover just next to my burning cheek.

"Gitte, did you see the tools they have?" Bitte said excitedly.

Lukas let his hand drop with a small sigh. Taken aback by the awareness between us, I turned my attention hastily towards my niece.

In her hands, she held out a knife with the blade first. I made a point of turning her hand so that the handle of the knife pointed at my stomach instead of the blade before I took it.

"Wow, what else did they use?"

"There are a drill and a lot of axes, too, but Bo won't let me hold them."

"They are almost as large as you," Bo said taking back the knife and laughing at her.

Bitte waved him off, "I'm much stronger than I look."

"I can attest to that," I said. "We always let her handle the bar brawls."

"We'll head out now," Bo said to Lukas.

"We'll go for a walk at the fjord," said Bitte. "Will you come?"

"Another time, little lady," he said with a smile. "I have to finish my work here."

"All right then," Bo said. "Let's go. See you later!"

"See you," Lukas replied.

I was just about to turn and follow the others outside when Lukas called me back. He held out his hand. I stared at it in confusion.

"I need my nail back, Gitte," he said amused.

"Oh yeah," I remember the wooden nail still clutched in my hand. I was reluctant to return it. "I've grown quite attached to the nail. How about I just keep it?"

He laughed again his deep booming laugh that made the air vibrate. "Afraid not."

"Can't I bribe you?"

Suddenly, he looked very uncomfortable. His eyes that had been fixed on mine shifted away. I didn't understand the change, but I knew that I didn't like it. Hastily, I took his hand and returned the nail. Then, because I couldn't stop myself, I went on tiptoes to give him a peck on the lips. It was clumsily done. Still, I felt my lips tingle from the rasp of his whiskers.

Before this could get any more awkward, I turned to leave. At the door, I cast a last look over my shoulder. Lukas was still standing where I left him gaping after me as if he couldn't figure me out.

"That makes two of us," I thought while I exited the workshop.

A snowflake fell on my nose when Bo closed the door behind me.

Chapter 5

"What does Stændertorv actually mean?" Laura, one of the Italians in my Monday class asked.

She had to ask twice more before I finally returned to reality. I hadn't gotten much sleep last night thinking about the awkwardness of every time I had met Lukas so far. For a while there I had been wondering about going back to the museum to search him out.

"And then what?" I had argued with myself. "Ask him out?"

Usually, I waited until the guy came around to doing that. Well, usually meant once. I didn't date. The realisation hit me. I didn't date, and up until now I hadn't felt left behind. Sure, most of my friends were in a relationship but I just hadn't felt comfortable letting someone else into my life. I knew why, too, and chose to ignore it.

"Stændertorv, right, sorry," I managed to rasp out. "Roughly translated it means assembly square, it was the square where the estates of the realm used to meet."

After class, I hastily snatched up my things to rush to the next class when Jorge approached me again.

"You seem distracted," he said. "I believe a break from all these lessons would do you good. How about a coffee. En kop kaffe?"

"Thanks for the invite. Unfortunately, I don't drink coffee."

A ridiculous answer considering the half-empty cup of the same liquid I had been nursing throughout the class. Jorge looked pointedly at it.

"Um," I cleared my throat. "This is strictly for medicinal purposes."

"Funny as always," Jorge laughed. "I won't give up, you know. See you on Wednesday."

"Bye."

I got off early from class this day. Papa and Julie had invited me to a family dinner. I was eager to go instead of spending a lonely evening at home. Ever since my flatmate had left for Berlin to spend the holidays with her parents, the place seemed strangely empty. Too empty for my wandering thoughts, anyway.

Julie opened the door. When she recognised me, a smile spread over her round face. She ushered me in immediately.

"Hi Gitte," she beamed up at me. She was a small and plump woman, her figure only exaggerated by the apron she wore around her stomach. "Come in, come in. Anna, Ditte, and Bitte are already there."

Sure enough, the whole bunch just seemed to have been waiting for me. As soon as I finished hugging everybody, Julie returned with a gigantic pot of meatballs in curry sauce and rice. It was delicious. Beat frozen pizza any day.

After dinner, we stayed for a little while. Papa talked about the concert they had been to. The two of them attended jazz concerts whenever they could. They went to folk dance events, as well. Ditte and I had been forced to do that when we were children, and I looked back in horror at my false step. Some poor boy always ended up with a bloody nose. Ditte's dance partners hadn't been better off. Once, she managed to slap a guy at a square dance. His nose had been cracked. From that point on, Mama took us out of dance class.

I searched out my sister. Judging by the long-suffering expression she cast my way, our thoughts had travelled into similar territories.

We made our escape not long after. Bitte was tired. Not yet ready to return home, I decided to walk the two of them up to the station.

"I actually wanted to ask a huge favour of you," Ditte said abruptly.

"Alright, but it will cost you," I teased.

"I have my ginger nuts ready."

"Ahah, that won't be enough this time."

"What do you want?" Ditte said resigned.

I pondered the question for a while, "Let's see. It's got to be good, too. Ah, I got it. You will watch 'Love Actually' with me on Christmas Eve."

Ditte groaned.

"You must be the only one in the world who doesn't like that movie."

"And I cling to my dislike. However, the favour is major. So, I accept."

They were just about to board the train when it came to me, "Hey, you didn't tell me what the favour was."

"You will come and babysit Bitte and Bo's daughter on Saturday."

Her smile as the doors closed couldn't have been smugger.

I reached for my phone and typed, "I will?"

The answer was immediate, "Of course."

"I'm not sure if biscuits and a movie cover this favour."

"Maybe not, but trust me, you will want to come."

On this ominous note, I put away my phone and rode my bike home. During the next couple of days, I tried in vain to get more information out of my evil sister. If she was good at anything, however, it was at keeping a secret. I ground my teeth in frustration as I usually did when I couldn't get her to tell me her secrets.

It turned out that she didn't want me to babysit the children at my place. Rather, I had to go to Bo's place to watch over them there. Since I was promised a full fridge, I didn't complain ... too much. So that's how I ended up in front of a building I remembered passing a hundred times on my way to the library with Ditte and the excited Bitte in tow. As it turned out, the two of them had already met Alexa, Bo's daughter, last Sunday. They must have hit it off, judging by the way my niece was dancing on her toes. Ditte rang the doorbell. I noticed how her cheeks were flushed, and not only from the cold. She was almost as happy as Bitte.

"She has a reason to be," I thought wryly. While I had to hang out with the kids the whole evening probably playing entertainer, she was in for a night out with her official boyfriend. The door opened. Inside, a flustered looking Bo stood ready to leave. Such an expression of utter bliss was plastered on his face that I was surprised, he didn't just spirit away Ditte and left me to my own devices.

"Come in, come in," Bo gestured with a welcoming smile.

We entered a large rectangular room. In the far-right corner was a built-in kitchen unit. As well as a dinner table. Straight on stood a sofa with a TV in front. Bitte threw off her clothes and ran through a small hall on our left framed by three doors. She disappeared in one of them. Squeals of delight drifted over to us. Meanwhile, I was impressed. Everything looked much better than my own flat ever since Conny, my flatmate from Germany, had left for Christmas.

"I thought I was supposed to be the tidy one considering that I'm the girl here," I said to Bo.

"I take that as a compliment," he winked.

"You know of course that it will be a mess by the time of your return," I warned.

"A mess?"

"Oh yeah, it's a special power of mine."

He blinked taken aback and probably trying to calculate the risk of leaving me to my own devices.

"She's kidding," Ditte laughed. "And there's Lukas to watch over them all, anyway."

I stiffened, "There's who?"

"My cousin, Lukas. You met him last weekend," Bo explained as if I would have forgotten whom I had been kissing so clumsily. "I thought it would be easier for the two of you to watch the children together. Didn't Ditte tell you?"

A couple of raised eye-brows were directed towards Ditte. She shrugged, "Must have forgotten."

Her sly expression told me otherwise. What are you up to big sis? At this moment, Lukas entered the room followed by Bitte and a little girl with a round face and rosy cheeks. She detected me. A blush coloured her face adorably. Looking up into Lukas' slightly less reddened cheeks, I noticed the resemblance between him and his niece. He didn't seem surprised to see me. I wasn't given time to ponder the question, though, before I was in his arms. It was a short hug, which my hormones tried to turn into a lifetime. I had hardly time to return it before he moved on to my sister.

Shortly afterwards, Ditte and Bo left to catch their movie or whatever they decided to do with their free time now that they had two lackeys at their disposal. The children kept us busy rather than the other way around. We played Ludo. I lost. We played cards. I lost. We played hide and seek. You get the picture. I lost, which surprised me. All odds were stacked against Lukas' tall frame, and yet I was rubbish at every single game. Or maybe it was my constant distraction by the same tall frame.

In the end, I threw down the cards in utter defeat.

"You lost again," Bitte chanted. I had to remind myself that she was my niece, and one simply didn't hit one's relatives. I opted for shaking my finger at her instead.

"Luckily for you, I'm a good loser," I bragged.

"You are really good at that," Lukas smiled.

"Thank you," I said before reconsidering the compliment. "Hey!"

"Can we go to the Christmas market now?" the two girls asked in unison interrupting further complaints on my side.

"We wouldn't have to cook," I said.

"I could cook," he answered.

"Is there anything you cannot do?" I said.

"A few things," he answered hoarsely, blushing again.

My hand hit the table, "I've decided, we'll go to the market."

And so, we did. Bitte reminded me to put on my mittens, Alexa pointed out the lack of shawl. On our way out, Lukas pushed my cap over my head and ears. Without a word, he strolled past me.

We went to Stændertorv. As soon as we stepped out of the flat, it started to snow. By the time we arrived at the market, a thin layer of snow covered the booths and the ground. The girls wanted to build a snowman but they only managed a tiny one since there wasn't enough snow. The market was small compared to what I had seen in Germany or even Copenhagen. In Berlin, there were several markets covering an area as big as the whole pedestrian street of Roskilde. We bought candied almonds, Bratwursts, æbleskiver of course, and hot chocolate. I cast a mournful eye at the glögg. Then, I decided to be a responsible adult. Well, not that responsible.

While Alexa and Bitte were looking for candy they hadn't had yet, I snug up on Lukas with a handful of freshly fallen snow. He was looking away as always when I put the snow on his head. He yelped and jumped back.

"Why did you do that?" he said in obvious shock.

"Revenge for calling me a good loser," I said with a smirk.

"You said it yourself," he argued.

"Did I? I don't recall," I said and turned to follow my niece and her new friend.

Unfortunately, I didn't anticipate a comeback, and there was a comeback. An ice-cold one down my neck. I squealed like a little girl turning around to face my foe. He wore the same smirk I had claimed for myself only seconds ago. Hastily, I collected snow to retaliate. However, he caught me before I could throw it at him pointing out the older man I was aiming my snowball of destruction at. True enough, the old man seemed to shake either with laughter or fear. His retreat was instant.

"Let me go now so that I might put this lovely snowball into your underwear," I said reasonably.

Lukas laughed tightening his arms around me. My arms were pinned to my side. His eyes weren't on mine again. But now they at least were on my face. On my lips to be exact. Heat rose all the way up from my toes to my cheeks.

"I don't think I will turn my back on you again," he promised. I felt his warm breath on my mouth. "Let me get you another hot chocolate to make up for being such a good loser."

I narrowed my eyes at him, "With cream."

"With all the cream you like," he grinned wiggling his eyebrows at me. I looked after him aghast. Had he just made a dirty joke? I must say, I liked the playful side of him. Maybe it meant that he was less shy around me. The thought made me grin like a lunatic. I watched his broad back move away from me to a booth. He was instantly followed by the two little girls. Somehow, he had them wrapped around his little finger while they only wanted to make fun of me. I grinned. Maybe it was because I was more of a child than an adult to them. Bitte certainly thought so.

"Hello, teacher! Fancy meeting you here," a voice said all too close to my ear ripping me out of my reverie of Lukas. I jumped, an appropriate reaction to someone startling you, I think. I whirled around to see the offender. It was Jorge wearing a huge grin that somehow managed to look innocent.

"Good for you that I haven't practised karate in years," I said.

"Oh well, I guess it might have been worth it. So, what happened to I don't like Christmas markets?"

"Oh, I'm just passing through."

He stared pointedly at my candied almonds.

"Never said I didn't like almonds now, did I?" I said with a sly smile.

He laughed, "Now that you're here, and we've magically met, would you like to grab a glögg. I could be persuaded to find a beer if you truly don't like glögg."

I shifted uncomfortably. Jorge was a nice good-looking man, but for one, he was a pupil, and secondly, no sizzle. Still, I didn't like blowing people off.

"Come on, Gitte. Have mercy on me as well as a drink."

He was standing a little bit too close his face tilted down to mine as if he would like nothing better than to kiss me.

"Gitte, who's that?"

For the second time in as many minutes, I jerked my head around. Why won't people stop sneaking up on me? There stood Bitte, a disapproving expression directed towards Jorge. Alexa was standing with Lukas a few feet away. Her face was directed towards the floor. Lukas' shifted between Jorge and me before landing at the cup of cocoa he held in his hands. My heart squeezed at the disappointed expression on his face. I knew it wasn't Jorge's fault. Still, I partially blamed him for that.

"This is Jorge, a pupil from my Danish class." Jorge raised an eyebrow at the formal introduction. "Jorge, this is my niece, Bitte, her friend Alexa, and ..." I paused unsure of how to introduce Lukas. After an awkward pause, I added, "Ahem, this is Lukas."

They shook hands. Jorge's gaze flickered between Lukas and me. He must have noticed some tension for he said, "I see."

I raised an eyebrow at him. His face was unreadable.

"It was nice meeting you guys. I'll head on, now. Have a nice evening. See you on Monday, teacher."

I didn't miss the accentuation of "teacher" in this sentence. With another wink, Jorge disappeared down the pedestrian street leaving an awkward silence behind.

"Do you think you've gotten enough candy then?" I asked in an attempt to sound cheerful.

"No," the two girls answered in unison.

"Well then, let's do something about that."

We followed the girls to the next booth with crepes.

"This has to be the last," I whispered to Lukas. "Else they will be on a sugar high all night." Lukas nodded handing me the cocoa he bought for me.

"Thank you, you're my hero," he exclaimed. "And you put so much cream on it, too."

He smiled slightly in answer. Soon afterwards, we headed home. The girls were tired even though they acted as if they could have gone on and on. Alexa even agreed to take my hand because Bitte desperately wanted to take Lukas'. I looked at them going ahead wishing it was my hand holding his.

"Is this Jorge your boyfriend?" Alexa asked.

"No, no, I work at a language school, and he's my pupil," I said hastily.

"He wants to be."

"You think?"

"Yes, he looked at you and smiled a lot."

"I see."

"Lukas likes you, too."

"He does?"

"Oh yes, I think he wants to be your boyfriend, too."

"How did you figure that out?"

"He is smiling a lot."

"Really, I didn't notice that."

"Yes, he does."

I know it wasn't advisable to question a six-year-old about her uncle, but I just couldn't help myself, "Doesn't he usually smile?"

"Not much."

The rest of the walk home was done in silence. We let the girls stay up for a little while getting all the sugar out of there system by watching a short cartoon. I said goodnight to them. I thought that maybe Bitte would be unsure whether she truly wanted to sleep in a bed she wasn't familiar with. But like Ditte suspected, my presence helped. Lukas tugged them in.

When he shut the girl's room behind him, it was still too early for Ditte and Bo to be back. They would probably get home in an hour or so. So, we sat down to watch some TV. It was a rerun of the Late-Night Show. I hardly concentrated on the screen. My attention was fixed on where my leg almost touched Lukas'. Almost, but not quite.

After half an hour, I couldn't handle the pressure, any more. It was either retreat to the other end of the sofa or reducing the space. I opted for the reduction of space. I scooted closer so that our legs finally touched. I felt his pressing into mine. Despite the clothes separating us, I felt his touch like a mark on my skin.

Lukas didn't move farther away. I took that as a good sign. He looked at me out of the corner of his eyes. I took in a deep breath and reached out a hand to intertwine it with his. He didn't pull away.

"Gitte," he said hoarsely turning his upper body towards me. "Who was the guy?"

A slight frown spread over his handsome face. He must have shaven at some point. There was the usual stubble but not a full-grown beard. His grey eyes were fixed on mine. A small blush tainted his cheeks, but this time I wasn't sure if it was out of embarrassment or something else.

"It's like I said," I sighed. "Jorge is one of my pupils from Danish class. He had asked me out a few times. I never dated him, though, if that's what you're worried about."

"Why not?" he asked quietly.

"Many reasons. The most pressing one being, not having time besides my job as the local superhero."

"Gitte."

"All right, no sizzle."

"Sizzle," he pronounced the word as if he had never heard it before.

His eyes fell on my mouth. His thumb drew circles on the back of my hand. I felt very much like a teenager before her first kiss. The thought of our nieces in the next room made me scoot away from him. He wouldn't let go of my hand, though.

"Do you ever see Sanne?" I blurted out the first thing I could think of to break the tension. His thumb stopped its slow circles, and his finger tightened around mine as he said, "No, haven't seen her in years. I don't even think she is living in Roskilde, any more."

"Makes sense, she always wanted to see the world."

"Both of you. You were always talking about it."

"That and boys," I sighed reminiscently.

"Do you still?"

"Still what?"

"Want to see the world."

I shifted uncomfortably tugging on my hand, which he wouldn't give free.

"I don't know," I said even though I did.

He caught my withdrawal from the conversation and blinked in confusion, "Gitte." His other hand reached out to

58

brush my hair away. There it was again. The tension. The awareness. The sizzle. I forgot what we were talking about. At this moment, my focus was on him, his hand in mine, his other hand on my cheek. Most of all his eyes. They were stormy like the deep-hanging clouds that sometimes covered the sky above Roskilde fjord. I always thought that I could touch them, they hung so low.

I found myself drawn closer again until the only thing I saw was the grey in his eyes before they seem to close on their own account. His lips fitted mine perfectly. The slanted closed-mouthed kisses upon mine caused my stomach to lighten up with electric charges. Sizzling indeed. My fingers drew the line of his jaw. I liked the raspy feel of his beard stubble. When his tongue tentatively licked across my lower lip, my fingers dove into his curls. I never even imagined how Lukas' constantly wind-blown hair would feel like. It was soft and thick, engulfing my whole hand. He moaned as I scratched my nails across his scalp. My tongue darted out to meet his. From there, the kiss turned frantic. We licked and sucked, bit and scratched, groaned and panted. The sizzle had moved further down my belly and in between my legs by the time his hand travelled from my hair to my bottom. He drew me closer until I sat on his lap. Something pressed uncomfortably into my hip.

I drew back and panted, "Don't tell me you are still carrying the nail with you."

I rubbed over the rigid dent in his pants. For a moment, he just looked surprised and yes, turned on. Then, he burst out with a booming laughter. I hastily pressed my hand on his mouth somewhat muffling the sound. I could still feel him shake with laughter beneath me.

Right at this moment, I heard the key turn in the keyhole. The door was pushed open. Ditte and Bo stepped in and stopped. I tried to imagine the scene from their perspective. Me sitting on Lukas' lap his arms draped around me and my hand on his mouth. I chanced a glance at him. His eyes were filled with mirth, whether from my joke or the situation, I couldn't tell.

I caught Ditte and Bo exchanging an "Oh my God!" gaze.

"Oooookayyyy," Bo finally said. "I'll go check on the girls."

He left Ditte to stare from Lukas to me and back again. Finally, Lukas took the hint and dropped his hands from my waist and bottom that he was still gripping indecently. Not without giving me a firm squeeze that made me squeal like a little girl, though. In revenge, I slid slowly from his lap making sure to rub the nail in his pants. He groaned before he could help himself.

"Please not in front of my eyes. I'm blind," Ditte complained in mock disgust.

I stood up gave a huge fake yawn and stretched my arms to the ceiling. "Weeeeeell," I drew out. "It's getting late. I think I'm going home, now."

"You do that," laughed Ditte.

Without looking at either of them, I put on my shoes and jacket. With a short "Goodnight." I was through the door. Snow was still falling as I hastily retreated from the awkward situation. The cold managed to cool my heat a little bit. The crunchy sound of boots tramping on snow appeared behind me. I didn't stop until a pair of arms came around my stomach effectively pinning me to a broad chest. I smelled salt and wood, a scent I started to associate with Lukas. Salt for the sea. Wood for the ships, the two things he loved so much.

"Gitte," his voice rasped into my ears making me shiver. "You forgot your cap, mittens, shawl, and bag."

"Doh!" I thought and turned around in Lukas' arms to face him. I couldn't stop myself. I started to giggle, at my forgetfulness, at Lukas and his hair sticking out in all directions after my hands had worked it into a frenzy, at being caught making out.

"So, hand your bounty over," I said.

"Or else?"

"Else I shiver you to death."

"Can't have that," he laughed probably waking the whole neighbourhood. I loved his booming laughter. Instead of handing me my property, he put on my cab and mittens. He slung the shawl around my throat using it to draw me closer.

"Let's get you home," he whispered his breath warm on my mouth.

I nodded reaching for my bag. We passed the ten minutes' walk in comfortable silence. His arm was draped around my waist keeping me close to his side. Although the night was frigidly cold, his tall frame sheltered me from the worst of the wind.

"How embarrassing being caught making out like a teenager by your sister," I finally voiced one cause of my awkwardness.

Lukas chuckled and squeezed me closer to his side.

"You're not embarrassed," I prompted.

"No," he said softly. "I'm too happy to be."

There was the sizzle again. When we reached the door to my building, it had grown to an unbearable pressure. My head spun as if I had drunk too much glögg when I looked at him. He leaned down to press a soft kiss to my mouth. My lips tingled. That decided the matter. I was just about to ask him up.

"I have to go home," whispered into my ear.

"Why?" I whispered back.

"I have to work tomorrow."

I could hear the smile in his voice. He loved his job. At the moment, I hated his job. I wanted to punish him for choosing it over my company. So, I nipped at his throat, trailed kisses along his stubbly jaw, and bit down on his lower lip causing a groan to resonate through his body. His lips came down upon mine.

Lukas was the one to draw back first. A regretful sigh slipped from his lips, "I got to go. There's a ship waiting for me."

"Ok, my Viking. Go to your ship then," I said regretfully.

He gave me a peck on my lips again that turned into another seething kiss. Suddenly he wasn't in my arms any more but stood a few feet away. I blinked in confusion. His smile was pained.

"I must go," he said. "See you soon."

"Yeah," I sighed turning around. Going cold turkey seemed the only way out of this situation. Before I could find my keys, his body pressed into me from behind.

"By the way, it wasn't a nail," he whispered.

I heard his footsteps retreat but didn't turn around. For a while, I just stood there letting the cool air soothe my burned-up state.

Chapter 6

"At the attic sat the elf dad with his Christmas treat,
His Christmas treat, so nice and sweet.
He nodded and he gobbled and he stomped his feet
'cause nothing's better than his Christmas treat."

I sang as loudly as I could, turning up the radio to full volume to the sound of "På loftet sidder nissen med sin julegrød" sung by John Mogensen. I loved the story about the little elf defending his porridge from the greedy rats begging to get a taste. I decorated the flat with twigs and small elves. I especially loved the one peeking out of a shoe filled with straw. A while later I looked around proudly. For once, the flat was neat and tidy. This was mostly due to the fact that I had had too much time on my hands during the last few days. Ditte and Bo had spent a lot of time together. Papa and Julie visited Alan in Aarhus for a few days. I had a short chat with my flatmate, but she wasn't there, either, to keep me company. So, instead of thinking too long about how much I wanted to see Lukas, I distracted myself with straightening the mess.

Now, observing the welcoming flair of my little flat I must agree, Ditte's obsessive cleaning had a point. I shrugged. That wouldn't keep me from making a mess in the future, of course.

"One cannot help one's nature," I told the empty room with a raised finger.

The only answer I got was another Christmas carol. I plastered a smile on my face and sang along. That's how I almost didn't hear the doorbell ring. A forceful knock made me think about my neighbours for the first time. I hope I didn't disturb them too much. Tentatively, I turned down the radio and opened the door. My shoulders slumped in relief at seeing my elderly neighbour Lone's friendly face. In her hands, she held a most welcome plate of goodies.

"Good evening, dear," she said. "I heard you singing. So, I came with biscuits."

"Just what I need to top my decoration session. Come on in. Do you want some coffee or cocoa?"

"Tea if you've got some."

"Naturally."

A short while after I placed a mug of steaming tea in front of her. I drank cocoa with cinnamon.

"Your decorations are lovely," said Lone.

"Thank you," I tried my best to smile with a mouthful of biscuit. "Is your family visiting for Christmas?"

"No, this year I will spend the holidays at my son's house. That's why I didn't bother to decorate."

"Sounds lovely. How many grandchildren do you have now?"

"Three. No wait, I forgot about the twins ... five then."

"You have a productive family."

"You could say that," chuckled Lone. "How about you?"

"I will be at my father's place again."

"And how about your plans for children."

"I have a niece," I offered.

"Wouldn't you like children of your own?"

The evil smirk tugging at my neighbour's lips indicated how much she enjoyed making me uncomfortable. Usually, I took intrusive questions like that in stride. At 27, I always thought people first started nagging you about children at the age of thirty. God, was I wrong. I didn't think people needed children to be happy. Most thought otherwise, which was exactly why I held my tongue, an exercise I wasn't really good at.

Lone obviously contemplated me. I never had any conflict with the older biscuit-baking lady, but I felt uneasy under her perusal.

To my relief, the doorbell rang once more. I jumped up eagerly – "Excuse me." – and rushed to the door letting whoever it was in without asking. I wondered if Ditte had decided to bless me with her presence after all. The heavy footsteps on the stairs told me otherwise.

At the first glance of a blond utterly wild head of hair, my heart started to jump painfully. The slightly downcast eyes and hesitant smile confirmed it.

"Well-well," I drawled. "I didn't know delivery men came in the shape of handsome Vikings nowadays."

"Only for very, very good losers," Lukas grinned back.

He arrived at my doorstep about to kiss me ...

"Hello there, I'm Lone, Gitte's neighbour," a delighted-sounding voice arose next to me.

"Fiddlesticks!" I thought. I had forgotten the lovely neighbour with a sudden interest in my private life.

Fortunately, Lukas seemed to have more manners than I. He stuck out his hand politely introducing himself. I wished that Lone would leave instead of staring at Lukas as if he was the finest piece of gossip she had ever found on my doorstep. I cast her a sidelong glance, which she met with a wink. I narrowed my eyes causing her to smile. The old lady knew fully well that I wanted her gone, but wouldn't do so until I spelt it out for her. She also expected that I was too polite to do that, in spite of my usual party mouth.

For a while, none of us did anything more than stand there. Then, Lone took the initiative, "Well, young man, don't you want to come in? We are having biscuits."

"Um, I actually have to ...," he began but was unceremoniously taken by the arm. Although Lukas was double her size, Lone pulled him over the threshold without breaking a sweat. He seemed too surprised to protest. By now, I was quite curious how this would play out. So, instead of helping Lukas escape I closed the door behind us and joined them at the table. Lone had just poured Lukas a cup of tea.

"You, young man, are you Gitte's boyfriend?" she was just asking when I sat down. I had to muffle a threatening burst of laughter. Not only had I never heard Lone call someone "Young man", but the question turned Lukas' head into an alarming shade of red. He cast me a pleading glance. I opted for immersing as much of my head as possible into my empty mug.

"Um," I heard Lukas' say hoarsely, "I am ... I ..."

"He's my workout partner," I interrupted the undignified stuttering. "I only ever use him for bed sport, though. Look at him, Lone. He might be the quiet type, but he's definitely packing some muscle there. Can you blame me?"

"No, I can't," replied Lone seriously.

"We often play games. He's the tall Viking warrior, and I am the princess whose castle is being raided."

"I see. What a nice game. My late husband and I used to enjoy similar activities," Lone winked and got up. "Well, don't let me keep you from your young stud. I have a meeting with my vibrator."

On that cheerful picture, Lone left the flat. I'm sure I heard her snicker on her way out. As soon as the door was closed, Lukas blurted out, "I can't believe you said that. I can't believe she said that."

I burst out with helpless laughter. Lukas' face had turned from red to green reminding me of a traffic light ready to explode.

"Don't worry, she meant nothing by it," I tried to soothe him. "And she has left, hasn't she?"

"Yes, she's gone," he said taking a sip from his mug to restore his nerves.

"Does that mean you don't want to play Viking warrior and princess?"

He hastily put his mug down, coughing. I tried and failed to look innocently back at him, "Just a joke. So, why are you here? Not that I mind."

"What if I told you I came for my towel?" he grinned shyly.

"I would tell you it's a lost cause. It is seeing someone else, now," I said regretfully. To be honest, I didn't have the faintest idea where the thing was.

"Fair enough," he chuckled. "Bo asked me to invite you to the Christmas party at Muse. My uncle will be there, too"

Muse was the community space near the station where locals and co-operators could organise all kinds of workshops, concerts, and other meetups. Papa and Julie were involved in some of their projects like the community garden and the annual jazz festival. I hadn't been there in ten years or so. I wasn't opposed to going, but one thing puzzled me.

"Why don't they just call me?"

"They have been visiting my uncle for a few days."

Now, that stung. Not only had Lukas solely sought me out to deliver a message, but Ditte had also gone on a trip without telling me. I couldn't help my face from falling.

"Um, I guess they also wanted to give me an excuse."

"Excuse for what?" I asked and thought, "Down, heart!"

"Well, um ... I guess ... an excuse to come by and ... see you," he said.

"God Lukas, you are a real charmer," I said turning red. "I'm glad you came by."

I stood up and let myself fall into his lap, which I remembered as a pleasant place to be. He watched me with his blush slowly receding. I loved to touch his stubble, to have it scratch my cheeks while I was kissing him. It stung but in a good way.

"How come you are so shy?" I asked quietly, almost in a whisper. "You didn't use to be."

He stiffened, but I just kept on stroking his face. He let out a deep breath before answering, "I didn't have a pleasant childhood I suppose."

"What happened? You were always quiet but not that shy."

"I was always quiet with you because," he gulped, "because I liked you." He closed his eyes for a long while before he continued, "My ... mother. She became an abusive drunk after my father left us. It was around seventh grade. At first, she was all right. Then, she wasn't."

I let my hand softly stroke through his hair to encourage him.

"My uncle took me in when I was sixteen. He's my mother's brother. He and Bo are my family now."

"What happened to your parents?" I asked hesitantly.

"I talk to my father now and then. He is living in Oslo. My mother ... I haven't heard from her in ages. My uncle talks to her, but I don't ask."

I thought about my own mother who I still missed so much that I kept on clinging to the rest of my family. I pressed my lips to his looking to comfort him, and maybe to be comforted as well. It was a long sweet kiss. I sensed that Lukas was holding back and pulled away.

"Your mother," he began hesitantly.

I immediately stiffened in his arms prepared to jump off. His arms tightened around me, the grey clouds in his eyes looked at me with understanding.

"I'm sorry," he whispered.

"Thank you," I mumbled, my gaze shifting away to the wall, which suddenly seemed very interesting.

"How about a movie?" he asked.

We moved over to the sofa. An animated version of "The Christmas Carol" was running. Throughout the film, I felt his arms around me pressing me into his chest. I breathed in the familiar scent of the wood he worked with and the salt from the sea. My belly tingled excitedly while my hand drew small circles on his stomach.

I stopped when I heard a soft snore vibrating through his body. Amused I looked at his relaxed face. His mouth slightly open, his arms still maintaining a strong grip around my waist. I tried to wiggle myself free, but they tightened. Without waking up, Lukas pushed us down onto the sofa. I snorted when he misused one of my breasts as a pillow uttering a soft moan of contentment. I would have preferred him in my bed, to be honest. Still, he was exhausted, and I wouldn't wake him. I turned off the TV, fumbled for a cushion, and closed my eyes. Unfortunately, Lukas was stroking me in his sleep. My skin responded to his touch. There was so much sizzling going on that I was astounded by his continuous slumber. It took me a long while to fall asleep myself.

Chapter 7

The sound of feet walking down the stairs woke me up. My right leg and arm were trapped beneath something heavy. I couldn't even feel them. My eyes seemed glued together. They were extremely hard to open. When I finally managed it, I was nonplussed to find someone lying on me. Then, I remembered last night and the unsatisfying end. He looked adorably peaceful with his hair all over the place and his mouth half-open. Judging by the wet feeling on my shirt, he must have been drooling.

My body shook with suppressed giggles. I couldn't keep it from bubbling out. Lukas grunted, "Why is my bed shaking?"

"Because you have been drooling on it," I said with suppressed mirth.

Lukas' eyes flew open. He looked at me in confusion. Then, he noticed the wet spot on my shirt. Before he got the chance to be mortified, I sealed his mouth with mine. Afterwards, he seemed to be more confused than ever. He sat up rubbing his face. My limbs finally woke up. It wasn't a pleasant wake-up call. I shook my right arm in an attempt to relieve the sting of blood rushing back into my veins.

"Next time, we'll take the bed," I said wincing.

"I'm sorry," Lukas smiled leaning down to kiss me once more. "What time is it?"

"Around 8 AM if my watch isn't mistaken."

A jolt went through Lukas.

"So late!" he said jumping of off me. He rushed to the bathroom. I heard the toilet being flushed after a few minutes. Lukas returned looking slightly more refreshed.

"You can use my brush," I said with a pointed glance at his hair. It looked like the home of a hedgehog.

"I did," he said with a surprised raise of his eyebrows.

His confused expression made me laugh. He shook his head at me, "I'm very late for work."

"So, no breakfast on the sofa?" I asked since I heard his stomach grumble indecently. "Have a biscuit. They are even better in the morning."

He took one with a smile. Hastily, he put on his shoes and jacket. When he bent down to kiss me, he was still munching on the biscuit. A few crumbs stuck to my mouth, and I licked them off, sensuously I hope.

He narrowed his eyes suspiciously at me, "Wicked princess. I'll see you later at the Christmas luncheon?"

I nodded. He walked out of the flat leaving behind his scent and a sense of longing in my chest. I had to fight the urge to run after him. Especially since I was late for work myself.

The rest of the day passed by slowly. Father Time wanted to mock me. I was sure of that. I taught a few classes throughout the day. Jorge hadn't tried asking me out again. He seemed to have moved his attention to Indah, the Indonesian girl. The coward in me was glad that I didn't have to explain anything to him.

During my break, I called Ditte. When she picked up, I started talking right away, "So, you've been visiting the father, have you?"

A sigh rose from the other side of the phone, "I knew I should have told you myself."

"Why?"

"I can hear that you're hurt because I didn't."

"Am not."

"Please, you don't fool me, little sis."

"Alright, a little, but that's my problem. So, how was the first date with the parents?"

"Ulrik is really sweet, protective of his son but sweet. You'll get to know him this evening. You are coming, right?"

"Yeah, haven't been to Muse in a while, though."

"Good, Ulrik is looking forward to meeting you."

"Me?" I was surprised. "why would that be?"

"Um, I got to go. Bitte is calling for me."

"Wait!"

"See you later."

She hung up. Something fishy was going on. I groaned in frustration. There was nothing to do but to wait for this agonisingly slow day to pass.

Evening finally arrived. I put on my favourite green dress, red pantyhose, and the obligatory elf hat. Combined with my Father Christmas shoes, I was satisfied with my reflection.

I hadn't been at Muse in a while. There were no fundamental changes. The community garden wasn't much to look at, at this time of year. I popped my head into one of the workshops. Someone was half-way through building an armour. On the wall hung a helmet and breastplate. I paid the entrance fee and had a look around the main building. The interior was stuffed with people, sitting around long tables, and chatting. The setting was cosy. Everybody seemed to know each other. Like a big family meeting. Usually, the smell of organic food filled the air. Today, I smelled sauce and butter and best of all, pork roast.

My mouth began to water. If I didn't find the others soon, my impatient stomach would wear me down. That's when I heard several voices shouting out my name. I scanned the crowd for familiar faces. Their shouting facilitated the process. Ditte, Bo, Bitte, Alexa, and Lukas were sitting in the middle of one of the two long tables. The girls, as well as Ditte and Bo, were calling my name. All the while, they were waving their arms through the air as if to shoo away a horde of wasps.

By now, the noise had quieted down. Every eye in the room zoomed in on me, their expressions expectant. I reconsidered my choice of wardrobe. In my elfish costume, I probably resembled some kind of entertainment. I hadn't practised my acting skills since fourth grade but I was willing to try.

"Silent night,
Holy night;
All is calm,
All is bright ... "

I paused. How was the rest of the lyrics? Damn my poor memory! "God bless us, every one!" I added in reference to "The Christmas Carol" I'd watched only yesterday, deciding to end my acting career then and there. Without further ado, I made my way over to Ditte and the others. Laughter broke out. Some people even clapped and whistled. I only looked up when I reached the empty seat between Ditte and a middle-aged man.

"Kill me with my fork," Ditte groaned as I fell into the seat.

"Not while everyone is looking," I replied. "This is your fault, anyway."

"My fault?"

"Well, mostly your fault. You made everyone look at me. You know I cannot stand disappointing the crowd."

Ditte snorted.

"That was great," laughed Bitte from the opposite side of the table. She had managed to squeeze herself in between Alexa and Lukas the sly genius. I caught Lukas' eyes. He didn't seem embarrassed. Quite the opposite. His smile nearly split his face.

"I must agree there," chuckled Bo. "Why didn't you try out for the community play in October?"

"Because she sometimes forgets to put on her socks and couldn't remember a line to save her life," Ditte muttered beside me.

I shot her a glare, which she returned with a smug smile.

"I can, too," I countered reminding myself of Bitte. I decided to forget the mittens laying at home. Probably on the sofa table, in one of my shoes, next to the sink, or beneath the bed. Besides me, the middle-aged man burst out laughing. I was taken aback by the vehemence of the sound. My questioning gaze landed on Lukas, then on Bo, who were wearing similar expressions of hilarity.

"Do you think I'm funny?" I asked my neighbour threateningly.

"Exceedingly so," he grunted breaking out into a gasping kind of chuckle.

"I'm not trying to be."

"Which makes it all the more delicious."

"Speaking of delicious, did you know that I eat old men for breakfast?"

"Do you call me an old man, little elf?"

He tried to look insulted. However, the corners of his mouth got in the way of his efforts.

"If I'm an elf, you must be Father Christmas, Old Man." I pronounced the last two words very slowly and loudly to exaggerate his age. We glared at each other for a while. Neither could hold it up. After seconds, we lay gasping over the table.

"I like her," he told the rest of the table still breathing heavily.

"Yeah," said Lukas with a slight smile.

I couldn't help a return smile spreading over my face.

"You are looking like a girl in love,"

I nodded convinced that my inner voice had made the statement. Wait, my inner voice didn't sound like a long-term smoker. I glared at my neighbour.

"I'm Ulrik, by the way," he said holding out his hand.

My mouth dropped open. I looked at Lukas and Bo in confirmation. The amusement on their faces told me that it must be true. I was rarely embarrassed, but at that moment I felt like a lit Christmas tree.

"The fork looks quite attractive at the moment, ha?" said Ditte, slapping me on the shoulder.

"Don't worry, Gitte," Bo attempted to reassure me. "You two are a good match. My father likes to tease."

I chanced a glance at the older man. He winked back.

"Rogue," I hissed.

"Through and through," he countered.

"I'm hungry. When can we get pork roast?" Bitte chimed in.

"Bitte!" Ditte reprimanded.

"Me too," Ulrik and I chorused.

We looked at each other and burst out laughing. The embarrassing moment was forgotten. Good to know that I wasn't the only childlike spirit around here. A short while afterwards, the food was indeed ready. We filled our plates with pork roast, caramelised and boiled potatoes, sauce and balls made of lentils. I filled my plate to the brim. Ditte scowled at me, then pointedly at Bitte. My niece eyed the stack of food on my plate with a calculating smile. Before I was drawn into the argument, I rushed back to the table. When they returned I was already busily devouring the small mountain.

"I like an elf with a healthy appetite," said Ulrik sitting down next to me.

I tried a smart retort but was forced to give up because my mouth was too full. Bo and Lukas returned with Alexa on their toes. The two men's plates resembled my own.

A choir sang softly in the background during dinner. I noticed quite enviously that most of them could remember the lyrics of "Silent Night". Oh, well. At least I could sing along at "It's hard to be a Nissemand". Bitte jumped up and persuaded all of us to join the group dancing around the gigantic Christmas tree in the middle of the room. I hadn't seen much of Lukas tonight. So, I was disappointed to see Ditte reach him first.

"Ditte, there's something on your blouse," Ulrik cried out to her directly behind me.

My accurately clad sister turned to him in astonishment. While Ulrik busied himself pointing out a non-existing spot on her blouse, I reached out and triumphantly clasped Lukas' hand. However, for the moment he was occupied with Bitte's constant chatter. Ditte reached my side shaking her head at Ulrik.

At that point, all guests had built a long line through the whole room. People started stamping on the floor in rhythm to "Nu' det jul igen",

"Now it's Christmas time
And now it's Christmas time
And Christmas's lasting until Easter
No that isn't true, no that isn't true
For in the middle will be Easter."

While we were singing, the line started moving around the Christmas tree and in between tables moving faster and faster. All the children were laughing, and I couldn't hold it back, either. In the end, almost everybody was sitting down or leaning on the tables to gasp for air. Ulrik strolled over to me.

"You don't mind since I am an old man, after all?" he said leaning himself heavily onto my shoulder.

"Not at all," I pressed out under the sudden weight.

"Ulrik," Lukas protested quietly beside me carefully extracting my body from his uncle's bulk. He slipped a hesitant arm around my waist but made no attempt to draw me closer.

"How about a little walk to the harbour?" Ulrik suggested with a twinkle in his eye.

Ten minutes later, we were on our way. We passed Stændertorv and Roskilde Cathedral. The church was built on a hill making it visible from almost everywhere in Roskilde. We took the way through Byparken down to the harbour.

Lukas' attention was preoccupied with the two little girls chattering on and on. Ditte and Bo walked behind me. I was left to walk with Ulrik.

"Ah, the boy doesn't have a clue," I heard him mutter.

He fell back and whispered something to Ditte and Bo. A minute later, they called Bitte and Alexa. By then, we had reached the harbour. Lukas and I stopped to look back. Ulrik waved at us impatiently.

"Go on, go on, Bo just wants to explain something about the museum to us. You'd be bored, I'm sure."

"Oh thanks," Bo said wryly. "Go on, we'll catch up soon," Ulrik made a shooing gesture.

Lukas looked at me with a raised eyebrow. I shrugged. I thought I had a good idea what the old man had in mind and was very grateful indeed.

Unfortunately, Lukas didn't seem to have a clue. None of us said anything for a couple of minutes. The harbour disappeared behind us. We entered a line of trees. I was shivering. Even though I had my hands safely tucked away in my jacket, the wind was biting into my cheeks and nose. I was glad for reaching the tree line because they sheltered us from the elements, at least a little. I sighed inwardly. Lukas was too shy to take advantage of the situation. Maybe he didn't care, after all.

"What's wrong, Gitte?" he asked next to me. His head was tilted towards my ear. The warm breath teased my cold flesh. I shivered and only partly with cold.

"Do you know why your uncle made us go on?" I asked hopefully.

He shook his head. Mine sank in disappointment. Lukas took hold of my arm pulling me away from the path between the trees.

"What?"

We didn't stop until the lanterns illuminating the path were hidden by the darkness of the surrounding trees. I heard him taking in a shivering breath.

"Do you want to be my princess?" he huffed out. I laughed. Not so clueless anyway. "Ulrik is a sly old man. He keeps telling me to be bold, but ... I missed you today."

"You were very busy with my niece."

"Yeah, if only she was a little older. Ouch!"

I had punched him. He was rubbing his arm. I couldn't see his expression. He wasn't talking. So, I grew unsure about his reaction to my teasing act of violence. A squeal resounded to the enclosed space when I felt two large hands gripping my butt. He drew me closer until there was nowhere we weren't touching. My feet brushed his. My knee pressed in between his legs.

I was craving to get closer to the hardness I felt pressed against my open thighs. My breasts and stomach rubbed his. My arms came around his neck. Our lips met. We kissed long and hard. My hands alternated between ruffling his hair and smoothing it down. His tongue massaged mine with deliberate strokes. I moaned into his mouth pressing closer. There was nothing to separate us save our clothes. I hated those clothes. They prevented me from feeling him.

I slipped my hand from his hair. A shirt was tucked into his jeans. I wrenched it out never breaking the kiss. He chuckled into my mouth while I just stopped myself from cursing in frustration when the shirt resisted. Finally, I had tugged it free. My hands fumbled their way beneath to feel hot skin.

"God, your hands are cold," he said half hissing half laughing.

"Hm," I moaned catching his mouth again.

I enjoyed exploring his broad back too much to care about how cold my hands were. Besides, they were starting to feel pretty warm to me. Soon, that wasn't enough anymore. I turned my attention to the front of him discovering a hard stomach and nipples that grew hard under my touch. I scratched them lightly with my fingernails. His answering grunt showed me how much he enjoyed it. So, I kept it up.

Lukas let me play with him for a while. But he didn't stay passive for long. His own hands were kneading my butt cheeks while I was busy pinching his sensitive nipples. Now, they travelled to the front of my dress, lifted the hem, and massaged my lower stomach with the same reverie as his tongue did in my mouth. I craved the wetness of his tongue as much as the strong fingers drawing ever closer to the most sizzling part of me. I'm sure I was giving out electric charges by now.

The exploring fingers reached the line of my pantyhose. He slipped one finger inside me causing my breathing to speed up in anticipation. He went slowly on purpose, I thought in frustration.

Deciding to return the favour, I popped the button on his jeans open and drew down his zipper. My hand discovered his length poking out of his boxer briefs. I enjoyed the hard feeling of him in my hands. He was as muscular as the rest of him. I squeezed receiving a moan in return.

All of a sudden, Lukas' fingers parted me. The first contact of him between my legs was electrifying. I jolted. By now I was so turned on that I thought I might burst from the slightest touch.

My hands grew bolder travelling up and down his length from root to plump top. The movement exhibited a low moan full of male pleasure.

He drew slow circles between my legs making me jerk in ecstasy every time he hit a particularly sensitive spot. Two fingers stroked me from my entrance to the sensitive knob of my clit.

"Wet," he said hoarsely.

"Aha," I moaned in response. "Don't stop!"

Our hands grew frantic, both of us seeking out our own release and the other's. In the end, they seemed to be intertwined. We were stuck in a spiral of lust. I didn't hear anything apart from Lukas' gasps and moans urging me on as much as mine did his.

Suddenly his hand was gone. He let the hem of my dress fall down. I still held him in a death grip.

"Gitte, the others are coming," he breathed heavily.

It took me a while to comprehend what he was saying. Meanwhile, my hand kept up the pace until Lukas couldn't hold himself back anymore. Before I knew it, he came all over my hand and his stomach. He tried to bite back the sound but a muffled grunt escaped him, nonetheless. The sight excited me so much, I almost came myself. As it was, I was aching fiercely between my legs.

"Lukas? Gitte? Is that you?" I heard Bo's voice coming closer.

"Shit!" Lukas cursed. Louder he said, "Yes, we're with you in a moment. Just wait for us!"

I heard Bo chuckle. Fortunately, his footsteps receded again. Lukas took my hand. His tongue licked at the mess he had made.

"Sorry for that," he said. "We'd better go back to the others. I have a better plan for our next play, though."

I forced out a laugh. I was still so turned on that I didn't know how I could wait. I couldn't very well tell the others to leave so that I could come as well.

"I'm so turned on," I sighed pressing my face into his chest. It rumbled as he answered, "I'm sorry, love."

Lukas found a crumpled tissue paper in one of his pockets and wiped himself from my hand.

We found the others waiting for us at the path not twenty meters from our make-out spot. This time, I imagined both of our faces blushing. Hopefully, I wasn't illuminating the path.

"What did you do in there?" asked Alexa with childlike innocence.

"Um," I began unsure of what to say for once. "We ... We ..."

"Squirrels," Lukas chimed in. I gave him a dubious look.

"Yes," I said slowly. "Um, yes. We followed a squirrel. Lukas is a big fan." I added this last titbit shoving my elbow into Lukas' ribs.

"That's right," he gasped. "I love them. They're fluffy and collect nuts. What's not to like?"

"Squirrels," asked Ditte doubtfully.

"Uh, can I see it?" begged Bitte.

"Noooooooooo," I said drawing the word out like a rubber band. "It was chased away by a big ugly snake."

Lukas snorted understanding the metaphors at once.

"Actually, I'm kind of tired," I said with a wink in Lukas' direction. "I think I'm heading home."

"Alright then, let's go," Ditte said to my utter dismay.

"What?" I sputtered.

"Bitte and I will stay at your place tonight. Didn't I tell you?" Ditte asked innocently.

"No."

"You probably just forgot. Ulrik is staying at Bo's place for the night, and I thought we could catch up over breakfast seeing that I haven't had much time in the last couple of days."

"And that's how thoughts about being left behind return to haunt you," I thought, resigned to my fate.

Our little group made their way back to the harbour. Here we would part, Ditte, Bitte, and I would take the route back through the City Park while the others took a more direct way to Bo's place.

"Will you go with them?" I asked Lukas.

"No, I live close by," he answered. "You could join me. It's not much, but it's home."

"I can't. Ditte has already made claims on my attention."

"Hm, I get it."

His downcast eyes told me that he was disappointed nonetheless. For a second, I forgot why I had to join my sister. Then I shook myself. Family must always come first. Even so, I rose on my tiptoes to press a soft kiss on his lips. As soon as my lips touched his, I forgot all about my obligations. I deepened the kiss extracting a moan from Lukas.

A throat cleared behind me. Embarrassed I drew back. There was frustration in Lukas' eyes but he couldn't press the issue. He was too shy. I, on the other hand, was an utter fool. I let myself be dragged away by my precious family. Ulrik gave me a squeeze and a sly smile in passing.

"I will see you soon, little elf," he whispered loudly.

"Not if I see you first, old man," I countered.

Later in bed, I couldn't sleep. The interlude with Lukas in the forest kept me from falling asleep. I thought about the frustration of never having a moment alone with him. There was always someone around. We both had our families and jobs. While I surely enjoyed working at the language school, Lukas was a shipwright through and through. He breathed his job. Bo had let it slip that Lukas spent way more hours at the workshop than he had to. If he wasn't there, he was busy building his own boats. He also attended a rowing club in the summer.

Lukas could have told me all that but he held back. Whether it was out of shyness or simply because he didn't want me to know, I couldn't say. All I knew was that I was drawn to him as I had never been to any other man. I liked to make him blush, to make him slightly smile, or laugh boomingly. I wanted to know more about what he had been through with his mother. Even more than that, I even felt an urge to talk about my own.

I fumbled for my phone and texted him, "Are you awake?"

"Yes," came the answer a minute later.

"Are you mad at me for not coming to your place?"

"No, but I miss you."

"Same here."

"I think the snake from the fjord has followed me home."

"Oh no, what will you do about it?"

"What do you suggest?"

"Petting is supposed to help with taming wild animals."

"I will try that. Do you want to meet up tomorrow?"

I hesitated before typing, "I'd love that."

"Good, I'll be there at 6 AM."

I blanched. My eyes must be deceiving me!

"I have to tell you right now that I'm not a morning person," I wrote back horrified at the early hour.

"I know."

"Well, as long as you know."

"Go to sleep, Gitte. It's midnight already."

"Bloody hell," I cursed my alarm clock confirming his message.

"Alright, I'll come," I wrote hastily. "But you'd better not touch that snake tonight."

"Promise, see you tomorrow."

"Tomorrow," I whined inwardly. "It's tomorrow already."

Chapter 8

An insistent buzzing woke me from a dream about small elves being chased by a big snake. Freud would have loved this. It took me a while to figure out where the sound came from. My alarm clock not only showed 5:50 AM, but it was also singing a Christmas Carol non-stop. I tried to turn it off. The button was harder to find than I would have thought, though. It took me two minutes to stop the annoying elf voices of the tune. At this moment, my phone buzzed with a message from Lukas,

"Pack clean underwear and put on warm clothes. I'll be there in ten minutes."

My bleary eyes needed three minutes to decipher the script. My brain then took one more precious minute to turn on the rest of my body. When I realised that Lukas would be here in five minutes, I sprang into action. The shower was lukewarm. I put on my favourite thong, jeans, and a thick sweater, threw socks and spare underwear into a small bag and rushed out of my flat.

Lukas was already waiting for me in front of the house. He took one look at me and shook his head. We went upstairs again. This time, I put on a shawl and my mittens. I also remembered to write a short note to Ditte explaining where I had gone.

"Dear Ditte, I'm off to never-never land with Lukas. Have my phone with me. Call if something comes up. Forgot to buy breakfast. See you on Sunday."

I chewed on my lower lip while I contemplated the message. I didn't like the thought of leaving without explaining myself properly. Oh well, I decided I would call her later. I didn't want to disappoint Lukas, either. He was already fidgeting and casting anxious glances at the door. So, I dropped the note in front of the room in which Ditte and Bitte slept and left.

It was cold outside, especially because I was still tired and shivering from lack of sleep.

"So, what are we going to do?" I asked yawning mightily.

Lukas smiled at my lack of restraint or maybe manners, "First, we'll go down to the fjord, and then I'll show you."

My heart jumped anticipating a repeat of last night's make out session. On the other hand, I would prefer a warm bed for that. It was still dark outside and would continue to be so for almost two hours. We passed the museum and the harbour and trotted along the fjord for what seemed like ages. I hoped that Lukas didn't plan on walking all the way to the open sea. That could take me a few days.

"Do you always get up that early?" I asked suppressing another huge yawn threatening to crack my jaw.

"Most of the time," he said quietly. "I like the feeling of being alone in the world. I like not hearing voices of complaint or demand. Right now, in the dark, I can hear my own thoughts, not what everybody else is thinking."

"I'm here, isn't that interrupting your thoughts?"

"Quite a bit," he admitted.

"What do you do while you are alone? What do you think about?"

"Um ... usually about how I can solve a particular problem with one of my ships. There's always something to mull over. I can think best when I'm alone. That's how I figured out that the nail I showed you a few weeks ago wasn't quite right."

"Oh," I said not knowing what to say.

"How about you?" he asked in a hoarse whisper. "What do you do when you are alone?"

I pondered the question for a while.

"Actually, I'm rarely alone," I answered. "I have a flatmate. Her name is Conny. She's from Germany. Usually, I'm around her a lot. She's spending the holidays with her family in New York. Anyway, I see Ditte twice or thrice a week, talk to my father just as much. My father's girlfriend Julie has three children. Two of them are living in Aarhus and one in Copenhagen. I also see them quite a lot. Then, I have classes and meetings with friends."

"So, when do you have time to think?"

"I take long toilet breaks."

Lukas burst out laughing. A murder of ravens flew into the air complaining loudly about the interruption of their sleep.

"We seem to be quite different," I said quietly after a moment.

In answer, Lukas snaked an arm around my shoulder pulling me into his side. I discovered that my head fit perfectly into the crook of his neck. I breathed in his scent. He smelled of salt as always but now there was the smell of soap mingled into the mix.

"I think we're quite similar really," he whispered into the darkness.

I almost didn't hear him over the rushing of waves on the shore only a stone throw to our right. I let myself be soothed by their sound and his declaration.

"I think I might like you a lot, Lukas Holm Eriksen," I confessed my voice muffled by his shawl. "I wonder why I didn't see that before."

"You were probably looking the other way."

After what seemed like an hour or more of walking, I wasn't shivering anymore. But my nose was numb from the insistently fierce blowing wind. The sky started to turn a lighter shade of dark blue. Birds awoke all around us. Most of them were seagulls and ducks, though. The rare lark made an acoustic appearance, too.

We reached a sandy beach. To our left rose a cliff high above us.

"I remember this place from my girl scouting days," I said. "We used to camp here sometimes. Later, we used to drink here ... a lot."

Lukas chuckled. He must remember, too, although he didn't drink a lot back then.

"I remember," he said. "Especially everyone swimming naked in the fjord."

"What?" I cried in outrage. "I didn't go to that party."

"No, I would have remembered that," he stopped to wink at me. "Sanne and you probably weren't talking again. It was her idea and we were all so drunk."

"You don't have any beer in that big backpack of yours, do you?"

"Sorry to disappoint you," he shrugged. "I also don't drink anymore."

"How come?" I asked in surprise.

For a while, he stared out to the fjord lost in his own thoughts. They weren't happy thoughts. His body had turned stiff and unyielding around mine. I nudged his cheek with my cold nose.

"It is what alcohol can reduce you to," he finally said.

I wondered if he was talking about his alcoholic mother. I put my arms around his middle and squeezed as hard as I could. Until he gasped and enveloped me in return.

He leaned down to whisper into my ears, "I need to get something before we can move on."

He extracted himself from me gently. I watched him striding away. He disappeared into a hut of sorts. I heard him rummaging around inside. The sound of something being dragged over a dirty floor met my ears. Curiously I tiptoed closer. Before I reached the hut, Lukas reappeared. Behind him, he dragged something that very much resembled a bath tub. A closer investigation revealed a small dugout canoe. I had seen similar constructions at an open-air museum in Lejre once. The boat was made of a single piece of trunk. Fire was used to hollow it out.

I watched with growing misgivings as Lukas pushed the boat into the water and gestured for me to join him.

"Did you build that yourself?" I stalled looking around for anything that might keep me from having to get on this boat. It was hardly longer than Lukas. I must have been braver as a child.

Lukas' scrutinised me as if he knew exactly what I was doing. I might have backed away, too. Suddenly he launched at me. I jumped back like a frightened rabbit. He caught me around the waist and lifted me into the boat. It bucked. Obviously, we didn't feel comfortable with each other at all. Before

I could jump right out again, the boat sank dramatically behind me when Lukas got on. The water around us was still dark. Judging from the few droplets I came in contact with, I didn't want to take a swim. Instinctively, I shifted back into Lukas causing the boat to sway precariously. Nevertheless, Lukas put one arm around me whispering softly into my ear, "We are going to play now. I'm the Viking warrior and you are the princess I have rescued. However, we will be out of danger only when we reach my home."

He handed me a row. I stared at it in confusion, "Since when do princesses have to row themselves?"

"They do it to impress their Viking with their strength," said Lukas.

I sighed. Lukas had already pushed us off the shore. So, I started rowing alongside my Viking. The sound of the sea made me smile despite the cold seeping into me. I managed to immerse the row at an odd angle a few times drenching Lukas and myself. Ditte would have laughed at me could she have seen.

"You know," I broke the silence. "I never was the best girl scout. I couldn't set up a tent to save my life. Whatever we built, I stumbled over it. Cooking duty wasn't much better. I managed to put half the camp out of order with my soup. How could I know that poisonous mushrooms looked exactly like ordinary ones, right?"

"Right," Lukas agreed loyally.

"We built a raft, and everybody got on. I decided to test the stability of our self-constructed vehicle by jumping on it like a trampoline. Not a good idea. A few kids including me landed in the water. God, they were angry. Suffice it to say that I didn't attend the girl scouts for long."

91

Lukas' booming laughter rose around me, "There must have been something you were good at."

I pondered the question, "There was. I could tie a knot like no one else." I looked suggestively over my shoulder and gave him a wink. He didn't seem to notice or mind that I was hardly rowing at all. The sky had turned a lighter shade of blue now so that I saw his face clearly. An air of excitement enveloped him. I wondered if it had something to do with being on the water again, which he clearly loved, or if it was my presence that caused his face to be split by a huge grin. I couldn't help but answer it. Maybe it was both. In any case, the wind didn't bother me so much anymore. His hair blew wildly around him. It framed his head like a halo.

Suddenly, the clouds parted to reveal a horizon that wasn't dark at all. Fingers of colour stretched out to touch each other. Blue, violet, pink, yellow and orange. The sun just poked its head out of the water. It was beautiful, round and shaped like a small red fireball. Its beam was directed at us so that we were enveloped in an orange-tinted light.

Without any regard for the swaying of the boat, I leaned back into Lukas. He put one arm loosely around me. A sense of peace came over me, which I hadn't experienced for as long as I could remember. When had I last stopped to take a breath like this? "Not since Mama," I confessed to myself. I had been wild and restless even before that, never breathing, always rushing on to the next distraction.

However, at that moment, I didn't need a distraction. The sun rose quickly. I watched it until it disappeared behind the clouds. Soon afterwards, it started to snow.

"That's what Simba must have felt like," I mumbled into Lukas' jacket.

"Simba?" he asked with a smile in his voice.

"From the Lion King. His dead father appears to him in the clouds after he had lost his way."

"So, you see dead people in the sky? Is that it?"

I slapped his arm and pushed away from him.

"Wherever you are taking me," I threatened, "we'd better get there soon. I'm grumpy without my breakfast."

Half an hour later, the picture of the sunrise was still imprinted before my inner eye. A weight seemed to have been lifted off my shoulders, and the smaller the shore behind us grew, the lighter I became as well. For once, I was content to keep my mouth shut simply enjoying the silence around me. My preoccupation led to me missing the patch of land that had appeared out of nowhere. When the boat came to a sudden halt, I stared in confusion at the grassy slope in front of us. Lukas brought the boat to its side and climbed out onto the bank. I followed him on shaky legs while he held the boat steady. It still shook like a pony desperate to see its rider on his arse. I managed to crawl ungracefully into the high wet grass. It was so slippery that I was afraid of falling right back into the water. Not Lukas, though. As soon as I had left our means of transport, he laid the rows into the boat and heaved both out of the water. I wasn't quite sure what to make of my current situation. Apparently, I was stranded in the middle of the fjord. The only reason I was here along with my only means of escape was just about to disappear behind the slope. With a sigh, I got up. If I had to be the princess in this scenario, I'd better not lose my Viking.

I slipped more than once while trying to climb the wet grass. When I finally reached the top, I was out of breath. So, I took a moment to rest and take in my surroundings. I suspected I was on an island, although my view was obscured by trees. The water between us and the mainland seemed far away. I only saw the cliffs rising out of a light morning mist. A stiff breeze blew around my nose reminding me of how cold I was. As fresh as the air was down here, I still longed for a place to warm myself.

Unfortunately, Lukas was nowhere to be seen. There wasn't a trace of a path either, and I had already admitted to being a bad scout anyway. The minute I entered the small forest, the wind eased. As a consequence, I felt a lot warmer. The bad news was, there was no sign of Lukas. I listened hoping to catch him walking through the trees. But I heard nothing except the constant rumble of waves and the occasional call of a seagull.

I wasn't used to being alone like this. Unease lifted the hairs on my arms. What if Lukas had left me behind? I started to make my way through the trees. They stood close together, their naked branches intertwining. I called Lukas. My voice echoed hollowly back to me. There was no answer. I was afraid of losing my way if I went any further. Leaning against a tree trunk, I tried to catch my breath. I told myself to stay calm.

"Don't panic," I told myself. "You're not alone in a place you don't know."

"Gitte?" I heard Lukas' call.

It didn't sound far away. I only had to unclench my jaw and answer.

"I'm here," I croaked.

A moment later, his windblown hair appeared among the forbidding trees. Concern edged into his face as soon as he saw me.

"Gitte, what happened?"

Not caring about how pitiful I must look, I threw myself into his arms. If my reaction startled him, he didn't show it. His arms pressed me closer into his chest.

"You're so cold," he muttered into my hair. "Let's get you warmed up."

I nodded. He took my hand and led me through the trees. I was wondering how he didn't get lost himself. To me, every branch, every root, and every thick trunk looked alike. However, Lukas seemed to find his way effortlessly. I was so relieved for having found him again that I could have kept on walking for hours with him by my side. As long as I wasn't alone, I didn't care a bit.

The walk wasn't long at all, though. We must have followed the invisible path for five minutes. I noticed the receding darkness of the forest. More light shone through the branches. The trees grew fewer and there was more space in between. Soon they made way for a small clearing. A house of sorts stood right in the middle. A cottage built of red bricks with a thatched roof. Two windows were in the front with white painted window frames. The door was also painted white.

"It looks tiny," I said with a sideways glance at Lukas. "Do you even fit inside?"

"I have to bend a little," he laughed, "But I do fit."

"It looks like the house of the witch in Hansel and Gretel," I said considering the cottage suspiciously.

"It's quite cosy," Lukas said. "Let me show you."

He opened the door. I noticed that the boat was lying in the grass nearby. Lukas had covered it with a canvas.

The interior didn't seem much larger than the outside. I must admit, though, it was cosy. The space was divided into two rooms and a toilet. The larger of the two rooms contained a sofa, a small kitchen with a sink, a fridge and two hotplates.

In front of the sofa was a fireplace. Every free space was covered with pictures of the sea and ships. Some were photographs, others had clearly been drawn by hand.

"I did like to draw when I was younger," I heard Lukas whisper hoarsely behind me.

"You made these?"

"Some of them."

He pointed to a drawing of the sea bathed in sunshine with just the barest hint of sail on the horizon.

"That's a very romantic painting," I said.

"You think so?" he smiled wryly.

I winked at him, "The princess is impressed. Is this your house?"

"My uncle's," he said following me into the next room.

There wasn't much to be seen except a huge bed that took in the whole length and width of the room. How did they even get it inside?

"Seems like your uncle has a taste for a romantic getaway as well," I laughed.

Lukas turned red, "Um, he used to be fond of his ex-wife."

I smiled to myself. To be thorough, I also peeked into the bathroom. In it was a toilet and a hand basin. Above the toilet hung a showerhead. I was used to such a sight from a few of my friends' flats in Copenhagen. Some old flats didn't use to have a bathroom. To save space, they had installed a showerhead above the toilet.

"There's more," Lukas said directing me away from the bathroom.

"You're sure? Better than the toilet?" I teased.

"I don't know how high toilets rank on your list of favourite things," he laughed, "but yes, better."

He pulled me to the window facing the back of the cottage. I expected to see only the dark forest. Instead, I looked upon a small lake glittering in the winter sunshine. A dirt path led down to where a green bench stood just waiting for someone to rest. A pair of swans drew small circles at the far side of the lake. I watched them apparently oblivious of each other. One of them lifted its head to look at the other one. It immediately stopped circling to join its partner. The awareness between the two creatures was visible even from this distance. I cast a sideward glance at Lukas and broke out in a grin when he lifted an eyebrow. My eyes returned to the swans. Now, they were circling the lake together.

A sense of longing overtook me. At that moment, I wished to leave this place, not to see the two swans that were so in tune with each other, even I could feel it. In equal measure, I never wanted to leave. They reminded me of Mama and Papa. So much so that my eyes started to tear up. As if they heard my thoughts calling out to them from over the lake, both of them turned their heads and looked at me. There seemed to be a challenge in their movement. I recoiled inwardly confronted with a truth I didn't want to face just yet, maybe never.

To ease the tension, I said, "Let's eat something." I turned my head questioningly, "You brought something to eat, didn't you?"

"Yes," Lukas said scrutinising me thoughtfully.

"Such a good boy scout," I patted his cheek.

We ate eggs and bacon, rye bread and cheese. Nothing had ever tasted better. After we finished our breakfast, it was still morning. So, Lukas decided to show me around the island. I found out that it wasn't an island at all but a promontory that reached far into the fjord. The lake was a small bay connected to the fjord by a shallow waterline, too shallow and rocky to sail through.

An hour after we headed out, snow began to fall. I watched it turn the landscape around us from a forbidding dark place to a magical winter wonderland. Snowflakes landed on my lips. I stuck out my tongue to catch a few of them. Lukas had gone on when I stopped to observe the snowfall. Now, I felt him moving back to me. My eyes closed while I was listening to the light crunching of his boots on the thin layer of snow. I imagined the salty smell of him surrounding me, the soft hair between my fingers. Before my inner eye, I saw a slight smile on his face, shy and almost not there at all. This was what the swan must have felt like. One felt the presence of the other in the air. With every sense, one reached out towards the other person. I had never thought about such things before I arrived at this deserted place. Maybe you needed to stand still to notice, not only yourself but also everything else.

Lukas had stopped right in front of me. He didn't touch me and still, I felt him. The air was buzzing around me. He didn't need to do anything. His presence was enough.

I couldn't have said how long we stood there, not touching, just breathing and reaching out to each other. When I opened my eyes, I wasn't surprised to see that his lids had been closed, too. Now, he opened them and studied me with an unreadable expression on his face.

"My parents had been together for fifteen years," I whispered. "They met at a Christmas luncheon when they both went to uni. Mama came from Germany. She was only supposed to be here for a semester or two. She always said that she didn't stay because of Papa, but I knew. I knew from the slight smile she gave Papa every time she said it. I knew."

Lukas nodded in understanding. I felt his sympathy, the sympathy I had avoided like the plague after my Mama died. I sighed. It was fine. The world hadn't ended or stopped to turn the other way. It was fine.

We went back to the cottage. I produced the cocoa from my backpack smiling triumphantly. We ate cold beef, potatoes and beans for dinner. Afterwards, we went down to the lake. Lukas showed me the bag of marshmallows he had brought. We made a fire, sipped hot chocolate and ate roasted marshmallows on sticks.

"I haven't done that in years," I exclaimed.

Lukas looked at me doubtfully.

"Alright, in weeks. But only because I have a little niece who enjoys sugar."

"Is that so?" he smirked.

"No," I sighed, "I'm a child within a woman's body. Satisfied?"

"I hope you're not too innocent."

"I am an experienced snake charmer if that's what you're playing at."

"I'm glad to hear that. There's one sitting right behind you."

His voice was so serious that I jerked around. I knew my mistake as soon as I saw nothing but whiteness all around me. Cold wet snow ran down my neck. Before I could stop its advance, it had reached my loose sweater. There was no escape. It ran all the way down my back. I screeched in horror, jumped up, and tried desperately to reach under my clothes to stop the wet coldness.

"You beast!" I screamed. "That's cold!"

Lukas was laughing so hard; his eyes were full of tears. He dropped his guard too, which was a big mistake. I threw myself at him two hands full of snow grasped firmly in my hand. While I distracted him with one, I put the other one under his shirt on his stomach. A satisfying high-pitched yelp

"Iiiiiick!"

"Oh, I hope I didn't unman anything," I said with an evil smile. Before he could recover, I jumped up and ran back to the cottage. I heard him throwing snow onto the fire. Shortly afterwards, his long strides followed me. When I reached the door, his arms came around me. But I was prepared. Another handful of snow dripped down his head. Instead of letting go, he pinned me to him rubbing his face into mine. Snow dripped down my face. I tried to disentangle myself laughing so hard, I couldn't stand upright anymore. He was laughing, too.

We just managed to get inside before we both collapsed onto the wooden floor gasping for air. Lukas lay sprawled on top of me. His shoulder shook with silent laughter. My own giggles subsided when I noticed how perfectly he was positioned, his legs on either side of mine, his pelvis rubbing against mine, his broad chest hovering over my breasts, his warm breath on my neck causing me to shiver with awareness.

He stopped chuckling to look at me. His eyes were black in the dark. His breathing changed from shakes of laughter to short inhalations of breaths. We were frozen in time. It seems as though the world had stopped to wait for me, for my move. My hands did what they had been dying to do the whole day. They dove into Lukas' soft hair. Pulling his head down. I didn't kiss him. Not yet. My lips explored his raspy cheek. I rubbed them against his chin, the line of his jaw, the dimple in his right cheek. I nipped on his lower lip, then his upper lip. Soon, he couldn't stand the teasing anymore. His lips caught mine. I opened my mouth instantly. His tongue dove in and out. My hands fumbled frantically for the zipper of his jacket. I broke the kiss.

"Undress for me," I demanded.

I felt rather than saw the blush on his face. He didn't protest, though. He stood up taking me with him. He bent down to help me out of my shoes before taking off his own. Before I knew it, he had lifted me into his arms and with a few long strides, deposited me on the bed. Then he seemed at a loss for what to do. I took over then, unbuttoning his shirt. He wasn't wearing anything underneath. Still, his skin felt warm to my touch. Excitement pulsed through me with every button I opened. I pulled it off as soon as the last button was open and slid my hands along his collar bone. His nipples pebbled under my touch. I bend forward to bite lightly down on one. His breathing sped up. I licked and nipped on the other one. My fingers fumbled with his jeans. He helped me to pull them down along with his socks. The only thing he was wearing was a black pair of boxer briefs. The dent in them was unmistakable. I brought my lips down to kiss him through the silky fabric. My tongue darted out to lick him from root to top. I took his head into my mouth still not pulling the fabric aside. The thought of how I would wet his briefs with my tongue made my stomach clench in the best possible way. He pushed restlessly against my mouth searching for more contact. "Oh fuck," he moaned. "Please take me into your mouth."

I enjoyed him squirming under my tongue. By now, I was at least as wet as his briefs. So, I obliged letting them fall to the ground. For the first time, I saw him fully naked. It was a glorious sight to behold. He was tall and hard all over. Not as hard as he was between his legs, though, I determined with satisfaction. Crisp hair encircled the root of his length. I rubbed my cheek against the woolly stuff delighting in the friction on my skin. The smell of salt and musk was even stronger here than anywhere else. My tongue flicked over his plump head. He tasted of the sea. Moaning silently, he arched into my touch. I took him alternating between kisses, nips, sucking and licking. I licked until he was drenched. I could have continued forever but he drew back looking down at me with drooping eyes. And then he gave me the four words I desperately wanted to hear,

"Let me fuck you."

My heart sped up, "I don't know. I'm a princess after all."

"I'll make it worth your while."

I considered him for a moment, "Prove it!"

He bent over me. His bobbing erection drew my gaze. I licked my lips. I never really wanted to taste a man's come so badly, but I found my nipples tighten at the thought of his taste. He helped me out of my clothes just leaving my thong and bra behind. And then he made it worth my while. His big hands enveloped my breasts kneading them until I wanted nothing more than his mouth on my nipples. I thought he would never get there when he rolled the peaks between his thumbs and forefingers. With agonising slowness, he positioned himself above me. I thought he wanted to make good on his promise to fuck me now. Instead, he let his muscular frame slide deliciously downward until his mouth hovered between my legs. He blew warm huffs of air onto my wetness. My thong must already have been drenched with my juices. I hoped he would rip them off. But no, his tongue darted out to lick me through my thong.

"Hm," I hummed watching him. He drew the line of my lips with his tongue sucking at the flesh. It wasn't enough.

"Ooh," I moaned when he came close to my clit but not quite close enough.

He gave me a mischievous grin.

"Bad Viking," I admonished huskily.

To my relief, his mouth came down on me again. He didn't lose the thong as I was hoping but his tongue still felt wonderful through the soft fabric. When I reached down to pull off the annoying cloth, he caught my hands.

"Come on Lukas," I panted. "Taste me."

His eyes flared, "Don't worry, I will. I have been waiting for this for a long time."

On that ominous note, he ripped off my thong and came down on me.

"Hm, yes, right there, don't stop," I moaned.

I couldn't help myself. He drew small circles around my clit before putting his tongue into my opening, fucking me with his tongue. My toes curled in delight. An unbearable ache spread through the place between my legs. My fingers scratched over his scalp again and again. I was so close. Before I came, I pushed his head aside. He looked up at me questioningly.

"I would like to milk you now, please," I panted.

He crawled up my body. My hands felt for him in the dark. I found his hard erection and squeezed it. When he was hovering over me, I took his mouth with mine tasting my juices on his tongue. I was so turned on my hands shook. Lukas ripped open a package of condoms and unrolled one down his shaft. I guided him to my entrance. He pushed slowly forward until all of him was immersed inside me. We stayed like this for a long while, just panting. I liked the feel of him filling me. When I squeezed, I felt him get harder.

"Fuck, that feels good," he moaned.

"You're not so shy anymore," I stated.

He chuckled shakily, "I seemed to have lost my shyness when you wet my cock with your tongue. Milk me, Gitte."

I did. We started off slowly. His strong hands were on my breasts as he rubbed deliciously in and out of me. One of his hands drew lazy circles around my clit making me feel emerged in my own lust. One of my hands stroked down his back while the other grabbed his butt cheek. My finger caressed his hole just as he was doing with my clit. His other hand pushed under my butt lifting me before he thrust himself harder into me. I cried out at the penetration. He moaned into my ear, the sound driving me crazy with desire. The combination of him inside me, his thumb between my legs, and his teeth pulling on my nipple sucked me underneath a wave of pleasure that suddenly rolled over me. But if I had to go, I would bloody well take him with me. As I gasped in ecstasy, my finger pushed inside his hole.

"Oh God, that feels good. I'm coming!" he moaned with pleasure.

He was growing even harder before his whole body shook with his release. It seemed to go on and on. Both of us were hardly able to move afterwards.

Chapter 9

Snow had started falling again. Thick round flakes covered the window seal and the ground outside. At some point, they fell so thickly that the eye couldn't see through to the lake, and the forest was nought but a barely visible shadow in the distance. The night was lit with millions of white dots chasing away the darkness. I watched the snow fall while I contentedly lay in the cocoon of Lukas' arms. He was sleeping his deep breaths as much a part of the night as the snowfall outside. His hair was all over the pillow. In sleep, he wasn't his usual tense self. His eyes were closed and his jaw relaxed. His mouth stood slightly open, and he was drooling a little. I smiled at the sight reaching out a hand to wipe it away. He opened his eyes. When he noticed my hand on his cheek, he smiled his arms tightening around my waist.

"Ready for another round, princess?" he whispered huskily.

"Lukas, I want to ask you something that might upset you, so beware!" I warned.

"Hm," he mumbled nestling my neck.

"Have you ever brought anyone else here?"

It was a ridiculous question, of course. Still, I didn't like the thought of sharing this place or this man with anyone.

Lukas leaned back but didn't withdraw his arms. He looked at me, a question in his eyes that I didn't feel comfortable answering. I already regretted having asked in the first place.

"Gitte," he whispered hoarsely. He was blushing again. I didn't like it, didn't like the embarrassment he felt, not in front of me. My finger reached automatically for his hair, the nails scratching his scalp. His eyes closed for a moment, and a contented sigh escaped him.

"I always come here on my own," he muttered after a little while. "I ...," he gulped clearly forcing himself to say the next words. "I haven't had a real girlfriend since Sanne."

I stiffened, "She must have meant a lot to you."

"At least I thought so at the moment," he admitted.

Jealousy reared its ugly green head. Wherever his shyness came from, it didn't only have to do with his mother.

"Tell me about her," I said.

He blew out a breath, "Well, you knew her. You knew she could be ..."

"A bitch?" I offered.

"Yes, that too," he laughed. "We were too young, I suppose. I felt lucky at the time that someone was interested in me. You know, I was this nerdy guy with glasses. My parents didn't have an idyllic relationship. They didn't notice me half of the time. So, I spent a lot more time with my cousin and uncle than at home. My father ... he always looked at me with this appraising gaze. Playing at being a Viking again? He used to say whenever I came back from Ulrik's. Ulrik used to be a shipwright, too, and I was fascinated by the models he showed me. At fourteen, I immersed myself in boat building. When I had to be home, I worked on carving small boats out of wood. That didn't keep me from hearing all their fights, though. They fought everywhere, at home, on the street. My mother started to drink back then. I just wanted to escape. Sanne offered me that escape. She wanted to be my girlfriend. We used each other, I suppose. We had sex too young. We were both fourteen. Afterwards, she would dump me every time I did something to displease her. More often than not, she just fancied someone else."

"But why?" I said. "Why did you let her do that to you?"

"I don't know," Lukas said, his hand ruffling his already unruly hair. "I needed the reassurance of having a girlfriend, I suppose. Like I said, my parents didn't get along. By the time I was fourteen, my father had abandoned us. My mother was left alone with her bottle ... with me. Now, instead of shouting at my father, she was shouting at me. I helped her carrying the groceries home, and she shouted at me for stopping to adjust the bags. I dropped anything at home, even a sock, she would grow mad. I went to Ulrik instead of home, she would let me have it. Mostly, she was angry about how much I looked like my father. I wasn't worth anything, nobody loved me, not even my precious uncle, I'd never find a proper girlfriend, I was destined for failure."

He stopped. His breathing had grown heavier at the memory. While he was talking, his arms had loosened more and more until they had completely fallen away from me. He turned on his back so that he was talking towards the ceiling instead of looking at me.

"One afternoon, I came home late again. My mother was sitting at the kitchen table waiting for me. She asked where I had been. When I told her, she called me a liar and came at me with a kitchen knife. I was so shocked, I didn't get away soon enough."

He pointed at a scar on his hip. It was a white line, not overly big but angry-looking nonetheless. I trailed it with the tips of my fingers, seething with the revelation.

"Luckily for me, she was too drunk to coordinate her movements. The wound wasn't deep, and anyway I was in too much of a shock to feel. I ran all the way back to Ulrik's place. I couldn't speak for a while but he got the whole story out of me eventually. After that, she got me out of there. The wound needed to be stitched. I tried to tell Sanne about it, but she was going on and on about something. I can't even remember."

"I think it was about her coffee," I said remembering the scene.

"Right, you were there as well. In any case, we didn't get back together, and I went back to being kind of a loner. I had the odd night now and then when I just couldn't stand being alone anymore. So, I went out to find someone to spend the night with. Whenever I thought I liked a girl more than staring at the wall, I heard the voices of my parents, Sanne's voice in my head, and I just couldn't make myself talk to anyone. That's why I haven't had a girlfriend in such a long time. I am damaged."

"You know what I think," I said forcing his head to look at me. "I think you're wrong about yourself. You have a wicked sense of humour, kids adore you, your family loves you, you are passionate about building ships, and the sexiest man I have ever met. And I'm sorry I never saw you as a child. I should have been there for you. I should have known."

He looked at me for a long while with uncertainty edged into the faint lines around his eyes and mouth.

"And you know what else?" I said taking a deep breath. My heart felt as if I had been running a marathon. "I really would like to keep you."

"Why?" he said wonderingly.

"Because I'm half-way in love with you already. Please, Lukas, let me fall all the way."

His eyes widened. He looked at me as if I was a strange species. Then, his face split in a huge grin as he said, "Fall away, love."

My heart raised faster at the endearment. I leaned over him opening his lips with my tongue. His arms came around me again. He pulled me onto him. I felt his hard erection between my legs. Wanting nothing more than to be filled by him, I reached for another condom and took him in hand sliding slowly all the way down until I felt his balls on my butt cheeks. He put two of his thick fingers into his mouth sucking on them. I watched him my stomach sizzling with anticipation. When he pulled them out, they were wet and glistening. He reached between us rubbing me from where he was embedded inside me to my clit circling the knob with unhurried strokes. I squeezed him inside me as hard as I could. His mouth caught one of my nipples while his right hand cupped my other breast. I mewled softly. My hips began to rise and fall in long hard strokes. Soon, I felt an electric charge every time I came down on him. He drove me fully wild when the hand kneading my breast travelled around me, squeezing my butt before circling the entrance to my hole. I never knew that could feel so good. I threw my head back. Even though I was unbearably turned on, Lukas always stopped short of giving me release. I pushed his head away from my nipple and bent down to take one of his into mine, biting it lightly in punishment. He was very sensitive there as I had discovered. Soon, he felt ready to explode inside me. But I wasn't prepared to let him come just yet.

"You are so beautiful, my Viking warrior," I panted. "You feel so good inside me, filling me. I want you to burst, to fill me with your spunk, your juices to mingle with mine. Let me milk you until you can't think anymore."

He groaned with pleasure at my words. He flipped me over so I lay on my stomach with my arms pinned to the mattress. One of his fingers pushed into my butt hole, the other caressed my knob with rhythmical brushes. All the while, he drove inside me from behind. At first, his thrusts were leisurely, but I discovered that they grew more frantic the more I mewled and thrashed beneath him. At last, I was falling. I clenched around him feeling as if we could never be parted from each other again.

"Oh god, Lukas, I'm coming so good! Please don't stop!"

"I got you, my Gitte," he groaned into my ear.

I imagined him spilling his spunk inside me on my butt, onto my breasts. His own release seemed to prolong mine. It took me a long time to wind down. Before I knew it, I had fallen asleep from the delicious weight of him, the pressure of him still firmly planted inside me.

Chapter 10

The morning broke brisk and cold. The cool air in the room made me revel all the more in the warm blankets around me. Last night had been a revelation. I had let Lukas into my heart. I loved him even though I hadn't told him exactly. There was no turning back. The thought scared me a little but I knew I couldn't turn away from this shy man that had opened up to me. My very own shy Viking warrior. I grinned at the thought. Who'd have thought that playing Viking and princess could be so much fun? I fumbled for his tall frame. My fingers returned empty. He wasn't there.

Immediately, I was wide awake. He wasn't in the living room, either, though a fire was burning in the fireplace. I threw on my clothes from yesterday and left the house. The snow came all the way up to my ankles. I found him sitting on the bench at the lake. Without further ado, I slid into his lap. He squeezed me to him.

"Do you regret yesterday?" I asked half jesting, half subdued.

"No," he answered rubbing my cheek with his nose.

"Are you sure?"

"I'm sure, love."

We sat there for a while watching the swans clean themselves or reaching for algae beneath the water.

"Are you in the mood for breakfast?" I asked finally.

"If there's something sweet for dessert," he said biting my earlobe.

"Possibly," I gasped.

We had breakfast first at the kitchen table. Then we had dessert at the rug in front of the fire. I always wanted to do that. This time, I took him in my mouth until he was shuttering with pleasure. While I was rubbing myself, I observed him bringing himself to climax. I grew hot just seeing his hand around his thick hardness. I never thought that a man stroking himself could be so arousing. I shattered with pleasure when I felt him coming on my breasts, his hands massaging his spunk into my skin.

We spent the day alternating between making out, playing in the snow like children, and drinking cocoa in front of the fire. We built a snowman. At least, it was a snowman until Lukas added two round balls for breasts. The day went by all too fast. The afternoon broke, and we had to leave. My heart squeezed painfully when the tiny red cottage with the thatched roof disappeared behind us.

Lukas was dragging the boat back through the partially melted snow. I followed him reluctantly. But we had to row back before it got dark. Tomorrow, we had to be back at work. Thankfully, the sun was still shining, somewhat relieving the sting of the cold wind. I almost hoped we would never reach the other side of the fjord. It had been so peaceful, just Lukas and me. Still, observing the perpetual lift of Lukas' mouth, I couldn't stay sad for long.

"Do you want to come over to my place?" asked Lukas when we reached the harbour.

My mood brightened. I nodded eagerly, my face breaking out in a gigantic smile.

"Of course, I want to," I began then caught myself, and added nonchalantly, "I mean, whatever."

Lukas broke out in his beloved booming laughter pulling me into him and warming me up thoroughly with a seething kiss. He lived in a small house with two rooms, a kitchen, and a bathroom in sight of the harbour. We took a long shower together, ordered pizza, and ate it watching a cheesy Christmas movie. By the time we went to bed, I could hardly keep my eyes open.

"Best Christmas ever," I mumbled into Lukas' chest right before I fell asleep.

Chapter 11

The alarm rang at 6 AM. I sat up looking wildly around.

"What, where, why, oooohh," was everything my scrambled mind produced before I fell back into a hot chest. Half an hour later, I was fully awake panting Lukas' name while he thrust himself into me from behind. An hour later, I was fully awake, and Lukas was late. He didn't look too distraught because of it, though.

We parted with a long kiss outside the museum. At least, we tried to.

"Hey strangers, where have you been?" A familiar voice interrupted us.

Lukas looked up still kissing me. He only drew away long enough to say, "Go away, Bo."

Bo's chuckle came nearer instead. I extracted myself from Lukas' lips if not his tightening arms. Bo stopped next to me scrutinising first Lukas then me with a smirk. Considering Lukas' shy nature, it should have been him squirming under his cousin's gaze and not me. I didn't know why I felt so uncomfortable but I did. Bo and Lukas seemed to notice my embarrassment because now they cast confused glances at each other, then at me.

"Lis has been looking for you," Bo changed the subject. "She's our intern," he added for my benefit. "It's seldom that she's in before you." Bo's eyebrows wiggled suggestively.

Lukas finally let go of me suppressing a sigh as he went, "Alright, I'll go and find her. I'm sure she only wants to see my nail."

A look of understanding passed between Bo and me before we burst out laughing. Lukas turned his back on us mumbling, "Such infantile behaviour."

He strolled towards the workshop where a young woman in her early twenties poked her head out to see what all the merriment was about.

"Well, I better leave for work as well," I said waving at Bo.

"See you," he called after me.

Today, I went to work with a spring in my steps. This was the last week of classes because Christmas was only a week away. We talked about Christmas traditions in other countries. Jorge was telling everyone how much he was looking forward to the Día de los Santos Inocentes on the 28th of December, a day for pranksters and costume lovers right after Christmas. Indah belonged to the big majority of Indonesian Muslims. Even though she didn't celebrate Christmas in the traditional way, she told us excitedly about how she would take the opportunity to be with her family. Kim from Germany amused us with stories of his little son taking off his scratchy clothes in the middle of the church to donate them gracefully to baby Jesus. We also talked about the Danish traditions of eating pork roast or duck, holding Christmas luncheon with lots of food before Christmas, lighting a calendar candle every day in December until the 24th, and of course watching "The Julekalender", a TV show with 24 episodes airing throughout the advent. I thought about buying a present for Lukas after work. For the first time since Mama died the Christmas spirit seemed to return to me.

I felt giddier to see him than I could ever remember being for anyone else. After work, I took my bike down to the Viking Ship Museum. Poking my head into the workshop, I saw the young woman, probably Lis, bending her head close to Lukas'. My heart made a painful jump as I saw them so closely together, even though I told myself that it was nothing to be worried about.

"Lukas, someone to see you," I gasped in surprise. Bo had snuck up on me from behind shouting into my ear. I held my chest in mock shock.

"Do you see that?" I glowered at Bo pointing at the ceiling. "That's how high I jumped because of you sneaking up on me like that."

He just smiled and winked.

Lukas came over to envelop me in a bear hug. God, my Viking knew how to give a good hug. I would have kept him for that only.

"Go home, Lis," he said over his shoulder. "You've worked enough for one day."

He didn't look around and therefore missed the amazed expression on the intern's face. She must not be used to getting off early. No surprise there. Lukas didn't come over as a strict teacher, but I was sure he tended to forget dismissing his pupils when he was engrossed in something. I was all the happier to see him leave his workbench for one evening because he would rather be with me.

"Hey wait, don't you want to come over tonight? Ditte will be there and the kids, it will be fun," Bo called after us.

We both just looked at him dubiously until he said laughing, "Just a joke, go on!"

We went to the fjord for a while just talking and watching the waves. The rest of the evening was spent in a mixture of eating, drinking, and other pleasant activities. Three glorious days we spent like this until my sister put her foot down. To my surprise, she told me that we hadn't spoken in days, and she wanted to know if I was still alive. I assured her that that was indeed the case, and she persuaded me to come over to Papa's place, whom I hadn't called, either. Guilt settled in the back of my head. So, I agreed to come. Bo would be there, too. Papa had met him the weekend before. Ditte told me that he was smitten since Bo wasn't above dragging out his limited experience with folk dance to get into his good graces. I asked Lukas if he wanted to come, but he told me that he had a surprise planned anyway, and that he would be working on that. This bit of information naturally brought out my obnoxious side to which Lukas was absolutely immune.

Nothing to do but to go to Papa's little soiree then. I was glad to witness the chemistry between Bo and Papa. They really hit it off.

"Careful there, sister mine," I warned with an annoyingly raised finger. "Papa is about to steal your boyfriend away."

"You're full of ...," she started before noticing her daughter's curious face and instead opted for, "ginger biscuits"

"Well, can't argue with you there," I winked plundering her plate without shame.

Later, I found myself doing the dishes with Bo. Unnecessary to say that this wasn't my idea. Bo told the others that he and I would be ever so glad for doing the dishes. I, my mouth full of confections, wasn't fast enough to deny him. That's how I ended up in the kitchen threatening him with soapy hands.

"I usually make a point of staying away from the kitchen," I sulked at him.

"Noted," he laughed. "I wanted to talk to you about Lukas."

I gave him a cautious nod, "Go on."

"He's told you about his parents?"

I nodded.

"He never said much about how living with them was. Ever since he came to live with Ulrik and me, he didn't talk much at all. I must be one of the people that knows him best. He was always the quiet sort. I'm glad the two of you are together. Ever since you started seeing each other, he is smiling. He used to live for his ships, even planning a rowing trip with the boat guild for three months next year. So, I'm glad that there's something, someone else in his life now."

"Yes, thank you," I said quietly.

He gave me an odd look, "Everything alright with you, Gitte?"

"Sure, thank you. I'm just glad," I pressed out forcing a smile.

His odd look didn't disappear. After dinner, I excused myself. I was tired and for once I wanted to be alone. I went for a long walk thinking about what Bo had told me. The indication that I might have changed Lukas' life in a small way made me uneasy but glad as well. What made me break out in sweat, however, was the news of Lukas' journey. He hadn't told me about it. Why should he? We hadn't been together for long. What made me panic was the thought of not seeing him, not having control of what happened to him, not having control of my own reaction. I had to see him. The harbour was lit with Christmas lights. Nobody was around at this hour. I don't know why, but I just had a feeling that I would find him here. I was right. When I knocked at the door to the workshop, the familiar dishevelled head of what was soon turning out to be my favourite person in the world appeared. His eyebrows raised as he took in my appearance. He was pleased to see me, but a concerned crease between his eyebrows soon replaced his pleasure.

"Gitte, what's wrong?" he whispered.

"Let's go for a walk."

We went down to the fjord where we had met again after so many years. Collecting my courage, I spun around to him, "Bo told me that you'll go on a longer boat trip next year."

He sighed, "Yes, that was the plan."

"What do you mean, it was the plan?"

He blew out a long breath before answering, "For years I wanted nothing more than to build ships and to sail them. I've lived in Norway for two years, spent a few months in Scotland, Ireland, Latvia. There's almost nothing I enjoy more than that."

I took in a breath trying to force down the lump in my throat, "Then, you should go."

He turned to me taking my hands in his and rubbed them slightly when he noticed my lack of mittens, "I want you to come."

"He wants me to come," a voice inside me triumphed. Unfortunately, my joy was repressed by a feeling of resignation because I couldn't leave Roskilde. I couldn't leave Roskilde. I couldn't leave Roskilde, and I couldn't watch him sailing away from me, either.

"I can't leave Roskilde," I said dully drawing my hands back.

"Why not?" he asked confused.

"I don't want to, and I'm not waiting for you to come back, either."

My voice sounded mean even to my own ears. A blush coloured his cheeks. I hated that it was me, my fault. "I thought this would be a short episode, anyway. So, we better end it now."

"Do you really mean that?" His jaw was set. He didn't look insecure any longer. He looked angry.

"Yes,"

"I love you," he almost yelled.

I didn't know what to answer. Pain ran through my heart. I was scared just as much of leaving him as I was of admitting it. So, I took the coward's way out. I turned on my heels and ran. I didn't stop until my door closed with a bang behind me. I fell on my bed trying to relieve myself by crying. My body deserted me, though. No relief for cowards apparently.

Chapter 12

It would appear, the heart doesn't know what it wants. I spent the next few days going through the motions. There were only two days of school left. In the evenings, I lay on my sofa not answering calls, trying desperately to tell myself that I had been right when I didn't know that at all. There was nothing right about this. The only one whose number I didn't read on my caller list was Lukas'. I missed him. Maybe he didn't love me after all. That's when I started to heat the leftover glögg from some Christmas party.

A sharp knock woke me up the next day. It didn't stop, either. I could just think of one person who wouldn't stop torturing me until I opened the door.

"Go away, Ditte!"

"I will not!" she called. "Open this door, right now!"

I ignored her. The key turned in my keyhole. Should have known this strategy would never work.

"God, Gitte! What happened to you?"

I turned my head into the pillow waiting for the tears to come. Nothing. I felt like exploding at any moment. Ditte sat down on the sofa next to me, "Scoot over you fat cow," she ordered gently.

There was silence for a long while. I didn't want to speak about the reason Ditte was stroking my back in soothing circles. Nor did I want to wallow, anymore. With a huge effort, I sat up, "Let's do something!"

If Ditte was taken aback by my forcefulness, she didn't show it. We watched a movie, some cheesy Christmas movie at the cinema. Later, we picked up Bitte from Tobias and went to Papa's and Julie's place. I didn't want to go home. While the others were playing cards, I was sitting on the sofa nursing a cup of tea. I didn't look up when Ditte sat down next to me.

"Do you remember the way Mama used to sing Silent Night in German?" I asked.

"No," Ditte sighed sadly.

"Neither do I," I started to sob.

Ditte took me in her arms rocking me slightly.

"I don't remember so many things," I choked out. "Her favourite food, why I was mad at her for reminding me how much of a child I still was, whether she read goodnight stories, whether she tried to teach us to speak German, how much she loved us. I don't remember. I only remember that I wasn't there. I wasn't there."

"Finally letting it out, are you?" Ditte whispered into my hair. "I hoped you would at some point."

"I broke up with Lukas," suddenly changing the subject.

"I know, why did you?"

"Because he asked me to sail away with him."

"So?"

"I can't, I can't leave Roskilde."

"Because of us," Ditte sighed. "Gitte, you have to accept at some point that what happened to Mama wasn't your fault. She would have died one way or another. Yes, you weren't there physically, but you have been there for her, nonetheless. You have to let it go. Stop hurting yourself. We're not going anywhere. We'll still be here tomorrow and the day after that. It's not your fault."

Suddenly, I felt myself being shifted from Ditte's arms to another chest. The familiar scent of Papa's cologne instantly relaxed me. He smelled of spices and most of all, the earth in which he was always rummaging around. The man loved his garden.

"I remember, sweetheart," he whispered softly. "I remember the way the two of you made plans for when you were older, how excited Lena was to have you study abroad. That's why she persuaded you to leave again despite her illness. Don't you think I've noticed, we've all noticed the way you have been clinging to us? And I'm sorry, I should have said something earlier, my sweet girl."

I wept into his chest for a long time. Ditte had left to help Julie with distracting Bitte. Finally, my sobs subsided.

"I remember how Lena used to sing Silent Night," Papa said softly.

"You do?" I sniffed.

"Yes, out of tune all the way through."

I was half crying, half sobbing while Papa rocked me in his arms.

"I know something that will cheer you up," he whispered confidentially.

"Yeah, what?"

"I'm wearing your bumble bee underwear."

"I'm not sure I'm supposed to know that."

Chapter 13

That night, Ditte, Bitte, and I stayed at Papa's and Julie's place. We slept together in one of the large double beds in the guest room. It was a sign of Bitte's advanced intelligence that she didn't bombard me with questions, although she must have witnessed my meltdown.

The day started off quietly. I was exhausted from last evening's episode, content to listen to Ditte and Julie talking about their plans for the upcoming Christmas Eve. Julie's children would come from Aarhus and Copenhagen. Ever since Julie and Papa had started dating five years ago, we always celebrated Christmas together.

Later in the day, Julie and Ditte were in the kitchen baking biscuits and preparing confections. I inhaled the delicious smell of cinnamon, nutmeg, marzipan, and chocolate. Papa was working at something in the garden. He had been caring for a family of hedgehogs, feeding the smaller ones so that they would make it through winter. I loved that about my Papa.

Whenever there was an animal in need of help, he stepped in. He also bought ridiculous amounts of bird food. This was probably the reason for a flock of a hundred birds currently making themselves at home in the jungle he called a garden, tweeting cheerfully away.

"My father, the bird charmer," I thought wryly.

I lifted my gaze away from the window. Bitte was sitting at the table with me. A concentrated frown creased her adorable face. I was helping her to write a Wishlist for Christmas. She had just started school a few months ago and couldn't write very well as of yet. That's how I found myself looking at her with an expectantly raised eyebrow, my pencil hovering in the air above a clean white sheet of paper. Well, no, it wasn't that clean anymore. I had currently made a list that included about 20 items. Everything from a ragdoll to numerous amounts of books, Lego, sweets, and a bike. I was wondering how many wishes one little girl could actually have. When I thought back to my Wishlist, at least the one that seemed to matter, there seemed to have been only one wish. In retrospect, this wish didn't seem to matter at all.

"What did you wish for when you were little?" Bitte interrupted my thoughts.

"I always used to wish for a knight in shining armour," I replied.

"A what?"

"A boy, I was wishing for a boy."

Bitte wrinkled her nose, "Why? They are stupid."

"So right," I sighed.

"So, why?"

"I wanted someone just for me."

"Why?"

"Because I thought nobody cared about me as much as I did for them."

"Why?"

"A good question. My Mama always used to tease me, and I was mad about that."

"Why?"

"Because I thought that it meant she didn't love me."

"Why?"

"Feeling therapeutic today, aren't we?"

"Of course," Bitte sniffed, but I could tell she was annoyed at the use of a word she didn't understand. After a while, she asked, "Gitte?"

"Yes," I said cautiously.

"Do you still wish for a boy?"

I pondered that question. I thought I had given up that wish alongside other childish dreams when Mama died. I certainly hadn't let anyone close enough ... until Lukas.

"Yes, I suppose so," I sighed.

"I like Lukas."

"Me too," I admitted.

"Then you should put him on your Wishlist."

I nodded giving my niece a sharp sideward glance. She returned it innocently. We finished her Wishlist. She proudly presented it to her mother.

"Feeling humble this year, aren't we?" she said sarcastically.

"Of course," said Bitte.

On impulse, I took the advice of my six-year-old niece when I thought that nobody was looking. I took a single white sheet of paper and wrote,

"Lukas, only Lukas."

I put it on the window seal alongside Bitte's Wishlist. For a while, I did nothing more than stare at it. The words became blurry when a single tear slipped out of the corner of my eye. My hand brushed it away. Through the window, I watched the sky turning grey. It looked like it would start snowing soon.

Before I could overthink it, I grabbed my jacket, called to the others that I would be back soon, and ran for all that I was worth. The harbour was at least a 20 minutes' walk from Papa's house. I made it in 10. I stopped in front of the workshop. The lights were on. My heart started racing. I almost turned away then.

"Don't be a coward," I admonished myself, determined to at least explain my reasons for running away from Lukas.

I took in a deep breath and opened the door to the workshop, just a crack. What I saw made the blood in my veins freeze to ice, figuratively speaking. The intern Lis was cuddled against Lukas' shoulder. Her head lay on his chest. His arms were around her, his hand stroking her back.

As soon as my heart started beating again, I wanted nothing more than to run off, run home, be alone with my heartache. I was too late. Damn wish lists to hell! I closed the door silently. At least that's what I thought. However, I hadn't taken two steps when it flew open again. Lukas stood there his face a mixture of surprise, anger, and something I thought might be longing.

"Gitte, what are you doing here?" he asked silently.

"Um." I started. As if I would say anything of my feelings now that I had seen him with someone else. "Sorry for interrupting. I was looking for Bo."

I could practically hear his teeth grinding together.

"Lukas?" Lis' head appeared next to him. I turned my head away not relishing the picture at all.

"Lukas, thank you," she said squeezing his arm with one of her delicate hands. "You really helped"

He drew his narrowed eyes from mine and forced a smile. I was relieved when her hand left Lukas' arm. She smiled tentatively at me in passing. Somewhere in the back of my mind, I registered her red-rimmed eyes. However, jealousy didn't allow me to think past her slim body in Lukas' arms, in my Lukas' arms.

"Um, since Bo's obviously not here, I'll leave you to it," I said feeling awkward.

"No," Lukas said.

"No?" I asked.

He gripped my arms, pulled me to him, and pushed us inside the Workshop. The door closed ominously behind us.

"I want to know what you're doing here?" he demanded.

I gulped, "Bo?"

"Gitte!" he shook me lightly.

"Alright," I said taken aback by his unusual forcefulness. "I came to explain my behaviour from the other day."

"You mean me telling you I love you and you running off like a coward."

"That would be it."

"Then why did you try to run off again."

"Let's think," I said sarcastically. "Might it have to do with the other woman in your arms?"

He didn't look happy about my answer, "Lis was sad about a fight with her parents. I was just trying to be a friend."

"Oh."

Lukas' hands fell off my arms. He turned away before continuing, "If all you're ever going to do is run, I'm probably better off without you."

"I know," I said trying to stop the tears threatening to run down my face. The explanation resounded in my head dying to be let out and, in a way, him turning his back on me made it easier. "You know that my mother died when I was around 19. What you don't know is that I wasn't there. I was in Scotland. When she was diagnosed with cancer, I wanted to come home. She told me I shouldn't. She had chemo and everything looked good. I didn't read the signs. My family, they kept them from me, but I should have known. The year she died, it was Christmas. I was too late to book a flight on the 24th, so I had to take one a day later. As it turned out, the one day made all the difference. She died before I ever talked to her again. She died while I was away."

I started sobbing again, wiping my nose with the back of my hand. By that time, Lukas had turned around to me.

"I said to myself that I wouldn't lose the rest of my family, too," I wept. "That's why I was so shocked about you leaving. I hadn't let anyone in for years and years, and there you were with your silent blushes, your raspy voice, and your bloody nail."

Before I knew it, I was sobbing into his chest. His arms squeezed me to him hard.

"I'm here, it's okay," he whispered making me sob even harder.

When I was finally finished, I looked up at him hoping that the heartbreak I felt wasn't too visible in my eyes, "So, you see?"

His tender expression told me that he understood or thought he did.

I let out a shaky breath, "I cannot be with anyone right now. You saw what happened. I hurt you because I haven't dealt with the past. Maybe I will never be able to accept you leaving me behind or me leaving my family behind. Travelling always means taking the risk of not being there on time. If you left me, and I couldn't do anything for you, my heart would break every day."

"Oh, my love, I understand," he said taking my mouth in a tender kiss.

I had missed him so much that my mouth responded automatically. Before I knew what had happened, my hands were in this hair, his on my butt. He ground himself unto me. Just one more time, something masochistic inside me chanted. His jeans were open in no time. The long skirt I wore was around my waist. We took each other on the working table. I took him in my hand guiding him frantically inside me. We gasped, pushed, thrust. I didn't let his mouth lift from mine for an instant. His finger between my legs sent me to a spiralling orgasm. He came not long after me. The whole scene didn't take longer than a few minutes, but I felt exhausted much like after a long day at work.

I was still kissing him long after we were finished, afraid of letting him slip from my life. At last, he pulled out of me, assisted me down from the table, and smoothed my skirts before zipping himself up.

I stood there awkwardly while he put himself to rights.

"Lukas?" I whispered.

He finally looked me in the eyes. I was taken aback by the determination I saw in them.

"No," he said. "I love you. Don't say that you're leaving me, now."

"I have to," I cried. "Didn't you listen? I'm too clingy to be with you. I couldn't see you taking off without me."

He let out an exasperated sigh, "I know."

"Then, you'll let me go?" I asked half hopefully, half disappointed.

"No chance in hell!"

"Stubborn man!"

"Call me what you want. It's not over!"

"I say it is."

"That's what you think!" he yelled back, bruising my mouth with a kiss. Before I even thought about pulling back, he let me go. I shook my head at him. My feet moved at their own accord so used to running by now, it was second nature.

"Love!" Lukas called. I turned back to a determined looking Viking bending over the table where he had just taken me. "Don't think you'll get far."

On this ominous note, he turned back to his workbench dismissing me. Furiously, I left the workshop, slamming the door behind me. Outside, snow had started to fall. With a last glance at the workshop, I nursed my broken heart close to my chest. No matter what he said, I couldn't let him sail away, I couldn't sail with him, so the only solution still seemed to be to let him go altogether. I let my head fall back, my tears mingling with the fluffy white flakes from the sky.

Chapter 14

What I like about Christmas: the smell of pine needles and freshly baked biscuits, oranges and clove, cracking walnuts, the taste of freshly baked biscuits, cocoa with cinnamon, glögg, the sound of bells, corny Christmas lights in the shop windows, forcing Ditte to watch "Love Actually", listening to the sound of "Last Christmas" for the hundredth time, a snowflake melting on my tongue, shaking a snow globe ...

What I didn't like about Christmas: missing Mama, missing Lukas ...

What I remembered best about Mama was that she loved Christmas. On Christmas Eve, she went all the way, baking biscuits although we already had enough to fulfil the needs of three families, dragging us to church although she didn't bother to go for the rest of the year, dressing us in funny elf costumes, which I loved and Ditte hated, dancing around the Christmas tree with us, a Danish tradition she embraced whole-heartedly. She also got Papa to play the guitar while we spent at least an hour singing.

Ever since Mama died, Papa tried his best to make Christmas as joyous for us as possible. For the first couple of years, we humoured him as best we could, but the joy of Christmas never truly returned. Only when Bitte was old enough did we start to recover. We could finally keep passing on Mama's tradition of writing wish lists, sprinkling sugar on top, placing it on the window seal for Father Christmas to pick it up. We cooked a big pot of porridge on Christmas Eve and let Bitte fill a small bowl for the nisse, the house elf. We would build a snowman with her, if there was enough snow left. We tried to continue every little thing that used to make Christmas special for us. In time, we began to feel at peace. When Julie came into the picture, she revived the singing session. That's how I found myself sitting squeezed in between Alan, Asger, his wife Rita and their children, Mads and Bianca, on the sofa. Anna was there with her boyfriend Rasmus, too. The room was buzzing with the sound of conversation when Papa appeared with his old guitar. Julie clapped her hands in delight. We all made a show of rolling our eyes but joined in the chorus of one Christmas song or another readily enough.

After church, it was time for presents. Papa shook his head with a wry smile over the elf socks I proudly presented to him. Bitte, on the other hand, was much easier to satisfy. She delighted over the snow globe as well as all the other presents she had received just as much as her cousins did.

"If one could just be as innocently glad for a present as a child," Alan sighed next to me.

"I don't know what you mean, I love Ditte's present," I said holding up the wall calendar she had blessed me with.

"Hey! You'll need it," chimed in Ditte. "You'd likely forget your head if it wasn't screwed on so tightly."

"And I hope you'll enjoy your present just as much," I countered.

She frowned at me, "You're not supposed to give out thongs as Christmas presents. Especially not to your sister."

We sang a few more songs until it was time for the children to be brought to bed. Afterwards, we sat there in companionable silence. During the rush of Christmas Eve, I was kept too busy to think about Lukas. Now when everybody was tired, I could hear the cracking of my heart like the walnut in Asger's hand. It was the silence that allowed for thinking and regret. At that point, there was so much regret. I just wanted to feel sorry for myself. Still, I was even too tired to feel anything but the heartache caused by my own stupidity. No matter which path I chose I felt as if I couldn't win. Therefore, I went to bed instead of meeting the questioning eyes of my family.

I was relieved when the next day began with laughing children happily playing with their presents. Julie had roasted a duck. There was so much food that I was wondering who was going to eat it all. We were a large family, but even so, there seemed to be enough to feed an army. My question was answered when the doorbell rang. I heard the familiar voice of Bo before I saw him. Even though it gave me a pang to see Bo when I had spent the whole night thinking about his cousin, I was glad, too. To my surprise, it wasn't only Bo. He gave me a hug before I could see the others being hurried inside by a hovering Julie. Alexa instantly ran off to find Bitte.

"It's good to see you, Gitte," he said affectionately before stepping around me freeing the view to Ulrik.

"Hello little elf," he chuckled. His hug was long, inappropriately so. I tried to clap him on the shoulder to sign the hopefully approaching end. Finally, he drew back, winked at me and followed his son. My heart jumped right up to the ceiling. There was only one person left standing in the hallway. Lukas.

I gaped at him. He gave Julie a hug. I thought about how good those arms felt around me anticipating as well as dreading the feel of him. However, I didn't need to worry. He just gave me a nod and followed his uncle and cousin. I stood there shell-shocked.

"Everything alright, Gitte?" Julie asked me with a slight frown. I tried to smile and reassure her. Judging by her lingering expression of concern, I had made a poor job of it.

"Let's eat," I said, attempting a cheerful tone.

The meal was awkward, at least for me. I couldn't help but stare at Lukas who was talking amiably with Anna and Alan.

"What do you think?" Alan suddenly asked me.

I blushed. Of course, he would assume I had followed the conversation seeing that I had done nothing but ogle Lukas the whole time while he was speaking. Oh, what the heck!

"It's definitely a good time to consider that problem seeing that it's Christmas. We could definitely use more love in the world."

Judging by Alan's smirk, I had made an ass of myself, "That's a noble attitude. So, you think that the streets between Aarhus and Roskilde shouldn't be so slippery, either?"

"Um, that's precisely what I think," I said trying to sound convinced while glaring at Alan. He had done that on purpose, the little bugger!

After lunch, Julie suggested we all grab our jackets and go for a walk down to the harbour. "Everything but that!" My inner voice yelled in self-defence. But I was outvoted. So, I tagged along staying as far away from Lukas as possible. I should have known better, seeing that his uncle had been trying to mindread me with his piercing gaze the whole day. We reached the harbour. Bo and Lukas showed the family around the Viking ships.

"Gitte, I want to show you something," Ulrik suddenly said.

He dragged me over to a small motor boat. I looked at it questioningly.

"I bet you wouldn't try to board it, little elf," he challenged.

I sniffed in disgust, "Is that a challenge, old man?"

"Maybe, little elf," he answered with a sparkle in his eyes.

I should have known. But I was a sucker for challenges. So, I boarded the boat hoping that the owner wasn't around. Triumphantly, I turned around to Ulrik. For some reason, he was grinning like an idiot. In horror, I watched him untying the boat. My mouth actually dropped open. I was even more astonished when Lukas jumped on causing the boat to shake precariously. I grabbed for his arms to steady myself. He took the opportunity to let his arms slip around me pressing a kiss to my half-open lips, effectively silencing every complaint. I couldn't believe it. I was being kidnapped!

My head jerked back. I cast an accusing glance at my family. They were all smiling like idiots.

"Bye Gitte!" Bitte and Alexa called after me waving wildly.

"I'm being kidnapped!" I cried. "Call the police!"

"We will!" called Ditte. "At some point. Now, it's time to enjoy yourself!"

"Papa?" My father would save me.

But he didn't. He winked at me with a look that said, "It's time, love. It's time."

Suddenly, the boat vibrated beneath me. Lukas had started the motor. My head alternated between his unruly hair and my cheerfully waving family. With a moan, I gave in to my destiny dropping down on an upholstered seat. We were sailing for a long time. I didn't say anything. Lukas didn't turn around. My thought played ping-pong in my head,

"Give in. You want him!"

"No, he'll leave me."

"He has kidnapped you."

"I can't leave my family."

"Your family wants you to leave. They just waved you off."

Without warning, the vibration beneath me stopped. Lukas had turned the motor off. At last, he turned around taking the seat next to mine.

"I'm sorry, love," he told me. "Of course, if you weren't such a difficult woman, I wouldn't have had to take such measures."

"You kidnapped me," I accused.

"Yes, I need you where you cannot run off while I'm trying to persuade you to be brave. I know you love me."

"Is that so?"

"Are you telling me you don't?" he asked, insecurity entering his voice. "If you're not in love with me, why did you come to the workshop? Why did you sail to the cottage with me? Why did you make me laugh? Why are you crying now?"

I couldn't help myself. The tear had slipped down my cheek before I even realised it, "I love you. It makes no difference, though. I'm still afraid."

He reached out a hand to wipe my cheek, "Won't you try? Won't you even try, love?"

I gulped. Would I? I thought about Mama, how much I wanted to have a boyfriend. I never thought the guy I'd fall in love with was Lukas, not in a million years. I looked up into the sky hoping for a sign. But signs were for corny movies. For once, I must decide on my own. I imagined Lukas a few years from now having truly left me behind. I was in the middle of my family, but they were distant because my growing bitterness kept them at arm's length. The picture I painted in my head wasn't pretty. It wasn't comforting. It was honest, though.

I took a shaky breath, opened my eyes, and threw myself into the arms of the man I loved, "I love you so much, it hurts. It hurts so much, Lukas. I love you, love you, love you."

I felt his body relax at my admission.

"Thank God," he said. "For a moment there, I wasn't sure. I have a present for you."

He pulled back just long enough to reach into his pocket and handed me ...

"A nail?" I looked dubiously at the wooden nail he was holding out to me.

"Not just any nail. It's the one you wanted to bribe me for. I'm giving it to you now. If you take it, you have to give us a chance. I mean, going on short sailing trips with me. Just a few days, in the beginning, nothing fancy. And I'll hold your heart hostage for as long as I want."

"That's blackmail," I cried out. For a long time, I took him in, my mind racing with indecision. There seemed to be only one relevant question to answer. Was he worth it? The more I thought about it, the more I realised how inconsequential my imagined fears were compared to the very real dread of not being with Lukas at all. And so, I smiled at last. The dear, dear man. I gripped the nail over his hand, "Challenge accepted."

At the same time, a snowflake landed on our intertwined fingers. My eyes shifted up to the sky. Apparently, the best wishes need time to be fulfilled, and one has to have the courage to accept what is given. I stretched my neck to give my Viking the sweetest kiss I had ever given anyone. He kissed me gently back, his hands framing my face. The waves were rocking the boat pulling us farther away from the shore. For once I didn't care, I would never write a Wishlist again.

About the Author

Lavinia Knop alias "Vinie Walling" is a self-published author of contemporary romance. During a student exchange in Roskilde (Denmark), she not only fell for Danish delicacies like glögg and æbleskiver but also one of the blond Vikings themselves, whom she is going to marry in September 2019. Vinie has written blog posts on cultural exchange, reviews on romance, and fantasy. Being partially sighted has made her appreciate black humour. Writing has made her describ e the world as a place full of wonderful cultural differences, unintentionally funny people, and lots and lots of romance.

To keep up with Vinie's latest news, visit her on her website www.viniewalling.com.

Author's note: I hope you found "The Viking on my Wishlist" an entertaining read. As a self-published author, I'm always grateful for feedback. Please consider rating and reviewing my book on https://www.amazon.com/dp/B07L1TKR8Q.